Kit McQuinn studied, and then taught, philosophy for many years in both the public and private sectors. He has published poetry (in numerous British and Irish periodicals) and philosophical articles on theodicy, freedom and personhood. Kit enjoys time in France, Italy and Ireland and is based in the English countryside, which he especially loves.

To David Hargreaves. Ever the best of friends.

Kit McQuinn

SIX MONTHS IN 1977

AUSTIN MACAULEY PUBLISHERS™
LONDON • CAMBRIDGE • NEW YORK • SHARJAH

Copyright © Kit McQuinn 2023

The right of Kit McQuinn to be identified as author of this work has been asserted by the author in accordance with sections 77 and 78 of the Copyright, Designs and Patents Act 1988.

All rights reserved. No part of this publication may be reproduced, stored in a retrieval system, or transmitted in any form or by any means, electronic, mechanical, photocopying, recording, or otherwise, without the prior permission of the publishers.

Any person who commits any unauthorised act in relation to this publication may be liable to criminal prosecution and civil claims for damages.

This is a work of fiction. Names, characters, businesses, places, events, locales, and incidents are either the products of the author's imagination or used in a fictitious manner. Any resemblance to actual persons, living or dead, or actual events is purely coincidental.

A CIP catalogue record for this title is available from the British Library.

ISBN 9781035820290 (Paperback)
ISBN 9781035820306 (ePub e-book)

www.austinmacauley.com

First Published 2023
Austin Macauley Publishers Ltd®
1 Canada Square
Canary Wharf
London
E14 5AA

To public libraries, everywhere.

Table of Contents

1. Moving Briskly On	12
2. Il Faut Reculer	32
3. Folsom Prison Blues	51
4. Fête	54
5. Chard House	58
6. Elodie	63
7. Symposium	68
8. The Roads to Freedom	73
9. Fatted Calf	78
10. Devil in the Flesh	81
11. First Night	83
12. Random Harvest	85
13. The Opposite of Murder	88
14. Planned Harvest	90
15. Judgment Day	92
16. The King Is Dead	100

17. After the Ball Is Over	102
18. The West	103
19. Last Days in East Haddon	109
20. Setting Out	114
21. Bloomsbury	117
22. Onslow Gardens	124
23. Soho	130
24. What I Call the RADA	134
25. A Family Affair	137
26. Berkeley	140
27. Oxford	143
28. Descartes	148
29. The Wallace Collection	151
30. Identity	153
31. Post	156
32. Dialogue	159
33. Blue Train	164
34. Middleham	169

Se moquer de la philosophie, c'est vraiment philosopher.
Pascal

We are lived by powers we pretend to understand.
Auden

1
Moving Briskly On

We have at last finished our A-Level exams, on the same morning. French Paper Two. James and I stroll illicitly from school into the village at lunchtime and have a celebratory drink in the walled garden of The Zetland Arms.

(Geraniums, sandstone walls, splashes of sunshine. So much more picturesque than the grey industrial village where I live just seven miles away. Where the pubs have flat roofs and Velcro carpets. And the cloudy sky is crisp-flavoured.)

Even though we are both now eighteen and wearing suits, I still expect James to be asked his age. But I needn't worry. His tendency to loudly declaim and to litter the conversation with middle-class references means the bar staff soon turn their backs or get on with cleaning glasses.

I, for different reasons, haven't been challenged for years. Maybe it's my rugby player build. Or my mask-like expression and saturnine looks.

Or my rather obvious intent.

He makes a valedictory speech without really meaning to, inserts a few abstruse words for my amusement. Our little game. He manages to jemmy-in, abiturient. Fair play. But then James can hardly finish a sentence without using words like feculent and exiguous.

He disguises his sentimentality quite effectively, but I can see he's already nostalgic for the last three years, the time since he first escaped Ampleforth to join me in the rural comp he has, against all odds, come to love.

Unlike me, he doesn't really care for ale, but sips it sportingly enough and pushes back his floppy public school mane at regular intervals. He lights a Peter Stuyvesant cigarette with his Dunhill lighter. Ridiculous. I slowly gather that it is the end of an era, the parting of the ways and all that.

Apart from the fact that he's off to Oxford in the autumn, I now learn he's been invited to the home of a family friend in Antigua for the next month or so. A friend of his father (The Winko). Another art dealer. He lets this piece of information sink in. I hardly need to point out that this will be quite a contrast with my holiday, which will be spent, like last summer's, in Ferguson's, the local car parts factory.

Last summer, Seventy-Six, was a real scorcher. I missed most of the light but caught most of the heat: the factory being unprepared for continental weather. But in the evenings I got to see the khaki-coloured fields, flagging trees and long shadows as I cycled or walked around the surrounding villages of gently undulating Northamptonshire.

(Very John Nash.)

James moves onto halves and airily reminisces (yet again) about his desperate flight from boarding school when he was fifteen. Gay and Catholic. (That old thing.) He never offers much detail and I certainly don't ask. Never have. The parental relief at his eventual safe arrival home was soon superseded by horror, incomprehension and exasperation. It was quickly decided (perhaps punitively) that he would go to the rather notorious comp in the next village and live with the consequences.

Whether this was an empty threat designed to get him back to Ampleforth or not, James seized upon it as a lifeline. He would live at home like everyone else and attend the local school. (Assiduously. Sedulously.) What could be more natural? (His parents' reaction to having their first-ever lodger goes unreported.)

Now, a mere three years later, he is Head Boy and has been accepted to read history at New College. He has made friends at school both despite, and because of, his perceived eccentricity. And he has a lover. A lad who left school after we did our O-Levels. A local mechanic and enterprising car thief called Jezz. (Who is, confusingly, engaged.)

James' life is sweet, at last.

His tone, unknown to himself, suggests that he has been on an unplanned detour, albeit a redeemable one, and is now back on track. Unlike the rest of us, he has a plan.

But for now, we just recount stories of our time together and compare our varying recollections. We talk excitedly over one another and laugh very loudly.

The locals glance over. They disapprove. So much the better.

(Who are they anyway? An estate agent who's banging his secretary? A defrocked vicar awaiting trial? A middle-aged woman who has just posted her first poison pen letter? Another of our games.)

As we talk, we retrace our steps, as if for future reference. Pinning butterflies.

My journey to Sedley Comprehensive School was less dramatic than his.

Sean, my eldest sibling, had gone to Daventry Grammar.

Eilish, Aisleen and Sheelagh went to the convent school, Notre Dame, in Northampton. Grainne, having failed her 11+ exam, went alone to St Mary's.

But then comprehensive schools arrived.

Redmond and I begged to be allowed to go to school in Rugby where a grammar school still existed. Mother implored, too, on our behalf. (After all, Dad worked there and could easily offer a lift in his newly acquired 1937 Austin Standard.) But no. Dad was a Labour man and comprehensive schooling was morally mandated.

No matter that Sedley was not really comprehensive and wouldn't be, couldn't be, for years. Redmond attended in its first and I in its second 'comprehensive' year. It had been and really still was a secondary modern. That meant lots of woodwork, metalwork, technical drawing and cross-country runs. (In the first year, we made pokers, bottle openers and ashtrays: the heraldic attributes of the working-class unemployed.)

Being there had felt vaguely like a punishment for an unspecified crime. A pre-emptive reformatory for the as-yet unformed. There was no Sixth Form. School leaving age was still fifteen and most left at that point; some through pregnancy. The unasinous teachers seemed either angry or defeated. Redmond was stabbed in the leg in his first year and bled a good deal rather than report it. Borstal rules.

Breaktimes were fight times. I beat up a boy two years older than me in my first week. Kudos. People were soon arranging my fights. It was hard to say no. (A sudden and heavy jab might start and end it. Or maybe a jab and a couple of hooks with some shouted advice to give up. People listen when their mouth is pouring with blood.)

And yet I remember reading the *Time Life* book on The Buddha in the school library when I was thirteen or fourteen and being inspired by the chapter on compassion and renunciation. I stared at the blue sky and cumulus clouds outside and contemplated life in a Tibetan lamasery.

Then I looked across the room at Louise Matthews, with her chestnut brown eyes, freckles and Pre-Raphaelite hair. And her short skirt and straining shirt.

Tibet would have to wait.

Northamptonshire County Council decided in 1970 that our village, Shenington, would benefit from an architect-designed new library. It was completely out of keeping with the vernacular, and so much the better for that. It was made of two adjoining octagons, with smoked glass walls and an inspired collection of books. Some faceless committee had decided that our village, notorious in the area for public brawls, spousal assault and juvenile delinquency, would benefit from more literacy.

The sense of affirmation this sparked in my young heart cannot be overemphasised. Seriously.

Over the last few years, my brother Redmond and I have virtually absorbed the place, albeit in unequal shares (his being by far the larger.) There was an unspoken division of labour. He had history and novels. I had philosophy. We both had art, biography and poetry. We have quietly and almost subconsciously worked our way through a range of writers. Our secondary school must have kept their own version of the Vatican Index.

For me, Schopenhauer, Sartre, Ayer, Camus, Koestler, Marjorie Grene. Introductions to the philosophy of religion, ethics and political theory.

Also, the plays of Eugene O'Neill, O'Casey, Synge, Beckett, Behan and Pinter. Classical Chinese poetry, translated by Arthur Waley. Modern poetry from Eliot and Stevens to Heaney and MacNeice. Alan Watts, Christmas Humphreys and DT Suzuki on Zen Buddhism. Edward Conze on Indian Buddhism.

Victor White OP on Jung. Biographies of Joyce, Pound, Yeats, Wilde, Collins, Markiewicz, Jung and Kerouac. FSL Lyons and Tim Pat Coogan on Ireland. Works by Aldous Huxley, Steinbeck, Laurie Lee and George Orwell.

We can recognise the styles of most of the preeminent western painters from Cimabue and Duccio up to Derain and Schiele and know a fair bit about their lives and times, too. More importantly, we love art, passionately.

Before I leave the library, I always skim the Oxford English Dictionary for recondite words to bait and amuse James with, and write them down.

Or find an obscure fact to bamboozle him with. And to sting him into retaliation, of course. (Our snarky put-downs are very much the point of this game, after all.)

It's important to me that my education comes for free. I've been a lefty since I was about fourteen. I covered my bedroom wall with posters of The Plough and Stars and the Irish Declaration of Independence and James Connolly. Dad always passes on his copy of *The New Statesman* to me.

In fact, throws it to me when he comes in from work (on the railways).

I catch it and start reading it hungrily, that second.

It must mean something that everything I learn in the library (or at home, for that matter) remains quite separate from school life. The person I am in the school is not me. I like it that way. Being invisible there. When in October I applied to read philosophy at university, a puny PE teacher I barely knew came up to me, grinning, in the corridor and told me he and some other teachers had just been having a laugh about it in the Staff Room.

I said nothing. I'm just a mutt. The educational equivalent of a hunger striker.

I once used the word signification in class and Mr Morris looked at me as if he'd caught me with my hand down someone's trousers.

Point taken.

So, thank God for Northamptonshire County Council in 1970.

The only stimulating lesson I can remember in school was given by a trendy student teacher in a black polo-neck sweater and tweed skirt.

She took us through some of Robert Frost's poems.

Electrifying. Transformative. Pharmacological.

Such a contrast with my usual English teacher, Mr Selkirk, from Blackburn—a fact that ferreted its way into every lesson. (Blackburn Rovers especially.)

I don't think he liked either the English language or children, so his careers teacher was either incompetent, sadistic or a humourist. I'd love to meet him. Preferably in a pub car park.

('You could of done better', Selkirk wrote on a piece of James' homework.

His mother saw it and became quite hysterical, apparently. Almost needed sedation.)

He punched me very hard in the chest one day. I was late to afternoon class, having been concussed in the annual staff versus school rugby match at lunchtime. I had scored the only and the winning try and the whole school watched.

Instead of letting me tiptoe to my seat at the very back and see me at the end of the lesson, he called me to the front and raged at me for being late. I could see he was acting. I was angry. Louise Matthews was only six feet away, for Christ's sake. When he finished, he said, "Now go to your seat."

I said, "You mean to where I was going in the first place, then."

He leapt up and swung a punch. Selkirk was well over six feet, but I took it and threw my bag at his feet and looked him in the eye. Silence. Both by now hyperventilating. He knew he might be in trouble. But he probably knew, too, that I would say nothing. I'm not middle-class.

(I just sound it.)

His mother was, according to him, the Best English Teacher of All Time.

(He proudly told us she returned, unopened, a letter he sent her as a student because she didn't like the way he'd punctuated the address. Sounds like an absolute cow.)

He took his marking home one weekend to the cultural rive gauche that was Blackburn and she asked to read our essays. She told him mine showed promise.

He wasn't happy. Either his estimation was right or hers, but not both.

Well, at least he told me. The utter cunt.

Apart from rugby, where I can be a handful (the tin shed, they call me) I've always been fundamentally alienated at school. It's not for me.

It's for someone I have no intention of being, that's all.

I'm the lady in the magic show who steps out unscathed, as daggers thud all around her. Except she receives applause, of course.

When I was fourteen or so, Aisleen invited Red and me to visit her at Westfield College in Hampstead.

Westfield is surrounded by gardens from a Rupert the Bear album: almond and magnolia trees, oriental ponds, bright green copper roofs, views across London, birdsong, avenues of plane trees, a beautiful library. And in the halls of residence, the bedrooms have sash windows and mahogany floors with cute gas rings on mock Iznik tiles. The corridors smell of polish and expensive perfume.

I was pleased to see one of my cubist portraits on Aisleen's wall: The Refugee.

The College was full of beautiful women. There must have been a bye-law that you had to look like Katharine Ross or Charlotte Rampling to get in.

Aisleen introduced us to her friends: French, Australian, English.

We went to the bar on Saturday evening, where students were dancing ecstatically to The Sweet and Showaddywaddy.

At school, we all go to some lengths to claim arcane musical tastes.

But these students were too cool to worry about what was cool. And we who cared weren't cool at all. We were bloody tragic.

In snatched moments over the two days, I managed to read quite a bit of *The Rebel* by Camus and Yevtushenko's selected poems. Aisleen was studying French and Spanish and mentored Red and me a bit, but without making a big deal of it. She found time to walk and talk with us on her visits home and encouraged us, wrote letters and sent books.

(I received one called *The Enlightenment*, in which I first read about Berkeley and felt a pang of aporia.) We are always greedy for time alone with Aisleen. She represents France, culture, ideas and escape.

(Cunning and exile. But with words.)

On Sunday, we sat in her room with three of her friends, playing wink-murder and laughing hysterically.

Aisleen and her friends had given us a glimpse over the wall and into an enchanted garden. There had to be a way back in. But not yet.

Redmond and I would chat as we kicked a ball around in the street outside the Working Men's Club next door to our house. One Sunday lunchtime, a squat old lady wearing a fox stole berated us for not stopping and picking up the ball as she passed by. I waited until she had gone partway up the sloping drive to the Club and took a shot at her.

The ball hit her squarely on the backside and she flew forward, spilling her Chihuahua as she landed spread-eagled on the tarmac. Redmond ran, and impressively fast; he was gone. I, always the slower thinker, stooped and waited for the ball to roll back to me.

As she arose, rubbing her hindquarters, she declared—almost as if opening a fête—that she knew who we were; that this was not over. With that, she entered the public bar.

But she never had that word with our parents, as she died in her sleep that night.

Redmond and I looked at each other expressionlessly when we heard, but said nothing.

***

Just before James first started at Sedley, the phone at home went on one Saturday and we learnt that Dad, who was picking up Eilish after an operation, had had a massive heart attack. He was critically ill in The Whittington Hospital in North London.

Mother and the older siblings went to Euston on the very next train.

Redmond and I were practically forgotten, and spent a lot of time sitting in the unusually warm Easter sunshine, listening to Lou Reed and David Bowie. We started experimenting with cooking. We stayed up late watching French films featuring Alain Delon, Jean-Paul Belmondo and Catherine Deneuve. We smoked a carton of Gitanes left at home by Aisleen's boyfriend, Jean-Luc.

When on an evening stroll along a country lane, a police car went past us, screeched to a halt and reversed.

"What are you two doing?"

"Discussing French symbolist poetry. What are you doing?" demanded Redmond, squaring up to him.

Go, Red.

After many weeks, we made our first trip to see Dad. It was a sweltering summer in London. Mother was there to meet us off the coach at Victoria Station. She was wearing clothes we didn't recognise.

"Do you want to eat first or see your father?"

"To see Dad, Mum."

(Right answer.)

We went straight to Archway. Dad now had a beard and looked like a kinder Hemingway. We found we had no words. We just sat on each side of his bed like good altar boys.

(The young man opposite awoke when we were there; Dad had been keeping an eye on him. He had attempted suicide and wasn't at all happy to have been winched, like the bellying kites outside on Highgate Hill, back to earth. They sectioned him there and then. Drama. After that, the visits grew more relaxed.)

Dad had finally stopped smoking. Instead, he would sit with his fellow patients at the end of the ward and play chess or cards. Dad's unbeatable at chess, and they all liked him. He seemed surprisingly comfortable with these men, many of them homeless and of dubious mental health.

He was warm and watchful. And different.

To Mum's obvious annoyance, he said that he felt he had briefly died and had a strong sense of there being no afterlife—even a sense of no God.

(I was interested in the possibility of experiencing a lack rather than a presence. Something I must return to properly at some point.)

What surprised me more than this disclosure was the fact that I thought he was relieved. Lighter in spirit.

We stayed at Eilish's basement flat in Stoke Newington. There were Republican posters on her walls (Ireland: The War Continues) as well as flyers for festivals and plays. She showed us a book called *Fire Words*, an anthology of poetry written by schoolchildren and compiled by one of her friends, another teacher.

We went to Irish pubs and visited Da some more. We saw an O'Casey play, *Juno and the Paycock*, at The Sugan Kitchen in Islington, a tiny pub theatre. London felt good. Hot, polluted, loud, messy, dissolute and bolshy. Good times, despite all.

Dad was indeed changed when he eventually came home. Before, he had been certain, strict, rather distant and decidedly pre-war. Now he was unsure, agnostic, more approachable, more open, perhaps a little more modern.

Our parish priest (who was Dutch) once joked that his Sunday prayers may have saved him. Dad replied that the vicar, Mr Courtney, and the Anglicans across the street had prayed for him too; maybe it was they who had saved him. He seemed to be making a serious point. Father Fabrius looked a little crestfallen.

Then James arrived on the scene. I had never been huge on friends. None of us had, having had each other. The family had implicitly frowned on the idea, I think.

He wore a posher blazer than most of us, which was a nicer blue, bought from Saunderson's in Northampton. (Yes, at school, the uniforms aren't uniform. Each version can be located on a class spectrum. Helpful.)

We got chatting in the dinner queue. He was impressed that I wore a waistcoat instead of a grey jersey. I was slightly amused that he shook my hand as he intoned his name, James Moncrieff. He spoke like Bertie Wooster. He was a Catholic. He was clever. He was almost certainly gay. He would obviously need looking out for. (James loves reliving this historic occasion and now even cites the time and date—both of which I forget.)

But the simple fact is, he really did need a friend, and fast, otherwise his last chance would have gone up in smoke.

He had to be made off-limits.

The first time I saw one of James' essays, I thought, *Jaysus*. What had we been doing? His Benedictine education meant that he was manifestly a few years ahead of anyone in our school. But not just that. He had been to Europe and America; even flown alone—and was allowed to smoke at home. He was practically a celebrity, for Christ's sake.

Of course, he made a few newbie errors. I remind him now, in the pub garden, that he needed some decrassification. (He squirms at this, but generously allows the term.) Shooting his hand up and saying, Please Sir! Please Sir! When a teacher asked a question—when everyone else was paring their nails, examining their split-ends or staring out the window. He soon learnt to keep schtum.

And early on, he walked across the invisible divide between the boys and girls in the schoolyard. He went straight up to a random girl—a completely innocent bystander—and, in front of horrified onlookers, asked her out on a date. This demonstrated his gayness beyond any reasonable doubt. Protesting too much. What the hell was he thinking?

(James looks blank as I relate this, but it really happened.)

As time went by, I realised that James actually liked our school. How could that possibly be? I'd fantasised about going to a school like Ampleforth.

There was clearly more to it than I understood.

He managed to acclimatise without remotely going native. A neat trick. When paying the modest fee for a day trip to Boulogne, he chose to pay, like the rest of us, in instalments. No one likes a swanky bastard with seven pounds to spare. (Though unlike the rest of us, he already had a heavily stamped passport, which almost ruined the effect.)

Some of the school's indigenous thugs even acquired a perplexed taste for him. A bloke who enjoyed light opera was hardly worth mauling, after all. And even if he did take a smoking jacket and velvet slippers on the field trip to Snowdonia, how did that harm them? Their decision to let him live even lent them a fleeting air of largesse.

But they still needed watching.

That field trip was fairly typical of us as fifteen-year-olds.

On arrival at a youth hostel, the custodian stood outside on our arrival, looking like Captain Ahab and solemnly proclaimed the expectations and high moral tone of the *YMCA*.

We stood in the rain, looking on blankly, apart from a couple of real villains who nodded approvingly. He then went in and upstairs. As we entered, Yacky broke open the charity box on the wall and emptied it into his pocket, almost as if he was officially collecting the week's takings.

We then lay on our beds, lit-up and started cursing the fucking hole.

We swigged vodka, which I, courtesy of sideburns, had bought in a Llandudno offy.

Within minutes, the place took on the feel of a concentration camp, the prisoners looking out of the streaming windows and dreaming of elsewhere. Anywhere.

We miserably learnt that Welsh pubs remained shut on Sundays and went for a walk instead. Georgie Coulter, a Belfast loyalist with an auburn moustache and NHS specs (whose party piece was to risk his life for no apparent reason) tried every vehicle on the road.

After a while, he jumped into an unlocked Volvo and let the brake off. As if it were paid work, we pushed it along the street, then down the hill and along another street, where Georgie neatly parked it and we continued exactly as before.

When we got back to the hostel, James was reading in bed and musing aloud that it was really only the Oxford comma that separated us from the animals.

James at least manages a smile at this one.

Soon after our return from Wales, James' mother drove us over to Stratford-upon-Avon to see *Macbeth*. (Yes, a big deal.)

At the interval, Mrs Moncrieff (call me Helen) asked me what I would like to drink.

"Jameson's please, Helen," I said. A slight pause, she adjusted her horn-rimmed specs.

"—And James, would you like something?"

"I'd like a Jameson's too, please, Ma." He successfully avoided her glare.

Another slight hesitation, then she sauntered up to the bar.

Helen had a Britvic orange as the two of us boys drank whiskey, as we all praised the brooding performance of Nicol Williamson. (I was beginning to drawl like Kenneth Tynan when the bell rang for the second half. Rush of blood to the head and all that.)

James now adds that his mother eviscerated him after I'd been dropped off. We both enjoy this image for a few seconds. He lights up again, pushing the fags and lighter in front of me, just in case I want to skank one.

Then onwards.

A couple of years ago, Redmond and I found work at The White Lion, a large pub and restaurant about two miles from home and overlooking the Althorp estate. Friday nights at the downstairs disco, Saturday nights and Sunday lunchtimes in the restaurant, waiting on tables.

We generally get a lift to work and sometimes a lift home (often with a drunk). Otherwise we walk, usually at one or two in the morning.

When we finally emerge for breakfast, Mother unfailingly says: *The dead arose and appeared to many.* This amuses her greatly.

Working behind the bar (our ages were overlooked) and collecting glasses is well-paid and quite good fun. The unfeasibly loud music is mostly Northern Soul. The bouncers are huge. The management crooked. The clientele soused.

If you are careful, you can do your work and get in a few smoochy dances and maybe make a date with a girl from Northampton; they are more fetching than most of the girls at school. And more amenable.

(One of them, Carmel Keenan, looks like Isabelle Adjani.

Sadly, she doesn't speak French. Or indeed, that much English, to be fair. But she makes looking like Isabelle Adjani go a long way.)

James eventually joined us on the payroll, getting over there from East Farndon on his Kawasaki 125, which he had (rather predictably) christened Lucinda.

Now and again the Shenington lads start a mass brawl, requiring police and ambulances. Glaswegian and Liverpudlian chefs make threats with knives. Affairs are had, scenes are made, cars are crashed and staff theatrically fired. Sour-faced Northern comedians appear at stag nights, as do surly strippers—one with a snake. We love it all.

One of my best moments was when a fight broke out—a big one—about twenty involved, plenty of glasses flying. I grabbed Laura Hayter and pulled her under the open staircase for protection. I don't think I tried to disguise my true motive. On the contrary, we were both entertained by it.

I'd never spoken with her, but she was in the year below me at school. I pushed her to the wall and put my hands against it, above her shoulders, as the fight raged behind me. She looked utterly calm and gave me the most delicious kiss. One that outlasted the scrap. It was the beginning of a largely mute but very intense set of encounters that went on for months. I think we both knew that words might easily spoil our innocent alchemy.

She would let me in the back door of her house after her mother, a nurse, had set out for her night-shift. Silent, urgent, unspoken exchanges.

The wine at The White Lion is called Hirondelle, the French for swallow (as in the bird).

James and I muse that this branding must have caused a few grins in some trendy advertising agency, swallow being the consumer guidance, presumably, for those understandably more inclined to rub the stuff on. This is a wine created for people unlikely ever to taste real wine, and more an inoculation against it. The antidote to wine, in fact. An industrial wine-substitute. But it sells quite well. We're all Europeans now.

About a year ago, I had read that passage from Sartre where the waiter (acting in bad faith) acts like a waiter, instead of simply being a man who happens to serve drinks. So I dropped the waiter act.

Interestingly, this was fastened upon soon after by a customer at one of our especially boozy bierkeller-themed nights. He seemed very keen to make me act like a waiter again, rather than be just some bloke who put a plate on his table. He required respect. Especially in front of his lady friend. We had a frank exchange of views. He invited me to discuss the matter outside.

I accepted. Then he declined.

The tyro existentialist perdured, for now at least.

I lived to Be another day.

Such is Finishing School.

I've talked more than usual and too much, though James always seems genuinely interested and often asks for more detail, as if storing it up for some nameless tribunal. And he remembers everything.

He unselfconsciously talks for quite a while about his time at public school. A kind of confession, but one without a plea for absolution.

He ends by saying, "I have to admit; I was a bit of a tart."

"A hoo-er you mean," I correct him, affecting my best Cork accent.

He smiles broadly. "Yes. A hoo-er! Even better. A bit of a hoo-er—"

***

2
Il Faut Reculer

I'll head down to Ferguson's and see when I can start. It's not a usual summer. Redmond is staying in London. In fact, everyone will be away, including the parents.

As Dad has now retired, they are (half) thinking of moving back to Ireland—either Cork or Mayo—and will spend the next couple of months there with family, looking around and weighing up the pros and cons.

I shall have the place to myself. I shall amass a great fortune and make a start on my reading list.

No worries and no complaints.

If Mum and Dad return to Ireland, it will be fine by me and I dare say the others too. It's always been a bit of a stretch for them, being here. And even for us, their children, though our parents don't want to hear it.

Home has always meant Ireland. To me, as a child, this was mildly confusing. Mum and Dad were metics. It was complicated, but we were essentially refugees, somehow dispossessed of our rightful inheritance.

England had set down lifeboats to lift us out of the cold grey sea, but our gratitude was tempered by the fact that it was

England that had also rammed our ship. (OK, so this is a bootleg version of history.)

We were also in a tight corner somehow: rather unwelcome and somewhat belligerent. Yet we were, in a stroke of cosmic irony, somehow superior to our richer, better-dressed, taller and more socially adroit hosts. We were kerns, princes, chieftains, rebels, princesses, not only from a different place but possibly from a different time, too.

We would find evidence of our true identity not in our rather arbitrary socio-economic circumstances, but in books, poetry, songs, dreams, conversations, catechisms, aspirations, imaginings, alcohol and, if absolutely necessary, psychosis.

If economic exile was the gateway drug to Celtic nostalgia, the habit was given a regular fix by visits home. The family farms, in Cork and Mayo, contrasted strongly and yet both provided confirmation of our true identity. Here our hidden selves had respite, and deracination gave way to easy acceptance and confirmation.

Were we like Persephone, living in the underworld and allowed to enjoy the sunlit land only sparingly? Were we hostages sent abroad as a tribute? Or Iphigenia, even, sacrificed to provide a fair wind?

The four farms in Cork were fertile and beautifully kept. Dad's elder brother, John Malone, had inherited everything, but his marriage was without issue.

Like me, Father was one of seven. We have plenty of relatives in Munster.

We often travelled by horse and trap and three or four of us would ride a Suffolk Punch around the yard. Our cousins in Cork were modest, kind, industrious and knowing. Being with them made me aspire to be like them. The girls were pale, pretty, blue-eyed and kind. The boys were handsome and spoke very softly as if to offset their emphatic masculinity. (The youngest, Jimmy, at fourteen, had decent sideburns and could handle both a tractor and a gun.)

When the Angelus bell sounded on the radio, everyone would break into prayer. Moments later, the gossip would resume, from the exact point of interruption.

Uncle Jerry took us to the dogs. (He bred greyhounds.) Sheelagh, Redmond and I explored Cork city alone, all aged under twelve, for hours on end. In those days, the old women dressed in black and wrapped up in woollen shawls. I don't think colour had been invented.

A goat could be seen sitting in the middle of the main drag. Schoolboys would catch eels from the bridge over the River Lee and keep them alive in tempestuous rain-filled potholes in the street. Shopkeepers, delighting in our English accents, kept us talking while other customers waited patiently. The centre of the grey city smelt dry and musty— the smell of the Murphy's brewery. And emblematically, in a glass case in the museum in Fitzgerald's Park, we discovered that most Irish of things: a white blackbird.

(This was almost a mystical experience for me. As if seeing something that, by definition, couldn't possibly exist. Stranger even than a ghost. More like a square circle. How I must have stared.)

In Mayo, the farm was much larger, wilder, poorer, but of greater rugged beauty. It lay at the head of a valley under the Sheeffry Hills and its river, the Erriff, offered plenty of brown and rainbow trout and the odd salmon. Fishing at night was called burning the river. This was the west and nights could be pitch-black, the gales roof-shaking and the rain torrential. I remember Mother pointing to an intermittent waterfall on the hills, spilling and pluming in a storm and saying *how beautiful* and my wondering what she could possibly mean.

But I soon learnt.

Grandfather O'Sullivan was irascible and constantly gave out. After coming in from the rain, he would stand in front of the blazing turf fire with his arms outstretched until so much steam flew up you'd think The Klan had planted a cross there.

Grandmother looked exactly like a squaw. She had grey hair and a long plait. Her skin was weathered and leathery. A lifetime in a house with no modern amenities suited her fine. She claimed to be descended from Grainne O'Malley, and may well have been.

Black and Tans had fired through the windows and threatened to shoot Grandfather during the last of the many campaigns Britain waged against those it unconvincingly claimed to be its own subjects. Granny and her only child, then a baby, had hidden under the bed until they drove off.

Over the years since then, all but two of her eleven children left Ireland, to return only seldom, but she was strong and glad to see people. She was agile on the rushing river's steppingstones and mocked those who hesitated.

Giving birth to her youngest, Aidan, had been difficult and the doctor would not leave her when called upon to attend another pressing birth a few miles away in the next valley: Granny's best friend. The woman died as a consequence, leaving her husband and several children behind.

Granny's dark eyes were full of intelligence and compassion. They said, I know it's terrible, but it's wonderful, too. She let me help her make butter and in the mornings I collected chickens' eggs from the dewy reeds, montbretia and long grass that surrounded the house, replacing some of them with eggs of clay. On a fine morning, we could see Clare Island. The turf fire suffused everything with the perfume of scorched earth.

Our cousins in Mayo, too, were impressive and like small adults rather than children. I compared myself unfavourably with them. Still do.

The extensive families in both counties were established and respected, known for miles around through commerce, church and school. Tribes and septs were still effective realities. Family and place-names were still patinated with social and cultural connotations. Not all of the earls had taken flight.

(Pat MacCurtain had had plenty to preach to us on the subject of identity, as we sat at the fireside in one of the farms near Mallow. His father, Tomas, had been murdered by the RIC and the killer was in turn shot dead by the IRA, which caused a pogrom in Lisburn.)

The inevitable return to England was painful. The Irish Sea was like the river Lethe, but instead of bleaching our memory, it bleached our status.

We were landless again.

***

England looked different after Ireland.

Like placing coloured cellophane over another colour to make a third.

In some ways, life was picturesque and leisurely. Mr Hayles delivered the milk by horse and cart. The horse defecated regularly on the street outside our house and two of our elderly neighbours (Mr Birch and Mr Andrews) would scurry out with shovels, keen that their roses should benefit.

This was, after all, Northamptonshire, the Rose of The Shires. On bright days, another neighbour, Mr Cooper, would sit on his doorstep, making shoes. Cobbling was a village tradition and there were two shoe factories nearby, which exuded the most wonderful aroma.

The population of Shenington comprised a few well-off farming families, some ex-bargees from the Grand Union Canal just a few miles away and a small number of long-established, consanguineous village families. There were no black or brown people, a few Irish families, and an Italian couple living in a dilapidated smallholding.

Mr Williams, at the farm across the street, employed as a farm labourer a German ex-Luftwaffe flyer, Andy Muller. He had been a PoW in the village and stayed on after the war. No one knows why. He still wore his black and maroon side cap and carried a flick knife he would flash open under our chins if we children asked nicely.

As I discovered later on, his knife was also used for skinning stillborn lambs and using the fleeces to pass off orphaned lambs to unsuspecting ewes. The ultimate assimilation.

We were Irish and Catholic; both identities marked us out for some as foreign and disloyal. Were we children at least English?

Au contraire. As someone once said.

To some degree, I think we accepted the idea that we were disloyal. Our true loyalties belonged elsewhere, across the Irish Sea. Mother was fairly fluent in (and often sang in) Gaelic, and Mass and Benediction were said entirely in Latin. English was, in comparison, a colourless language. England was a country without a culture and a godless, soulless place.

Unconsciously, we were perhaps like sleepers, biding our time—inarticulately dreaming of an unlikely revolution. England had not been kind to Ireland; that much we knew and consequently adopted a policy of quiet insubmission.

Hadn't we land and even a family castle, elsewhere? And hadn't we the one true faith and the ability to sustain ourselves without the help or approval of our polite but uncomprehending neighbours? (The English media, from cartoons and TV bit-parts to popular comedians, presented us with the idea that we were stupid. But to us, this was seen as just a tiresome price to be paid. A levy on blow-ins like us.)

Weren't we manifestly, even embarrassingly cleverer than most of our classmates?

(Nearly all of us, including me, had outrageously advanced reading ages.)

And anyway, didn't we too, often laugh at the quainter Irish expressions and paradoxes? (Is it yourself? You can't get there from here—) And didn't we make each other howl with our own Irish impressions?

I had been born with the cord wrapped twice around my neck. It was unwound briskly and calmly by the family GP, Dr Simms.

After noting my yellow jaundice, he commented favourably on the pleasing shape of my head, a compliment I was to cleave to later on, when compliments proved rather hard to come by.

The previous night, my eldest sibling, Sean, slipper in hand, forced those who knew how to pray, to pray. I understand that before leaving, the doctor intimated to Father that seven was quite enough. *The best wine was left till last*, Mother would later say to me. Or maybe the best because the last.

The rackety house was on three floors, on the edge of the village by the pre-Reformation church, St Etheldreda's. Bedrooms were shared, alliances formed and strata demarcated. On the walls hung an image of the Sacred Heart of Jesus and a couple of sepia photographs of Galway Bay. There was a font of holy water by the door.

The bulky gramophone was ludicrously out of proportion to the tiny collection of records that stood inside it: Gigi, Count John McCormack, Maggie Barry, A Nation Once Again. Not much else. But singing was normal to us and an air started two flights up would often be continued by someone downstairs and then completed by a third.

Watching a Hollywood musical required little by way of suspension of disbelief; what could be more natural than leaping about and bursting into song? *The Sound of Music* came out when I was six or seven and we instantly knew and sang every song, identifying unreservedly with pre-war Austrian aristocratic emigrés. The film was more or less about us, wasn't it?

The toilet was outdoors, about forty yards away, past the chicken coop where we would feed the peckish inmates with dock leaves, en route. There was no central heating at home and in the winter, ice would form inside the windows.

Bedtime was accompanied by yelps as we leapt between the damp and freezing sheets. There was no indoor bathroom until I was about six. The coal fire was eventually replaced by a gas fire, which was seldom turned on, and then never fully. It heated an area the size of a suitcase, at most.

On Saturdays, we each received a three-penny piece and would race to the sweets shop to spend it. On Sundays, we would each be given a square of Fry's Chocolate Cream as a treat. Much of our food was grown in the garden or the allotment. We had no phone. We had no car (until I was eight or so). Father cycled the ten miles to work in Rugby each day, arriving home around six in time for supper alone with Mother in the kitchen. We respected this seemingly romantic arrangement and stayed well away.

Laughter was loud and frequent, but not because our jokes were especially funny. Perhaps we were just naturally primed to laugh.

We were dark—not unlike gipsies. We almost invariably won class prizes. We were athletic, meeting all the expectations of victory in track and field. Father would take a day's leave for school sports day and clap his huge hands modestly as we collected a shelf-load of silverware.

I once returned from the County Finals and handed him two First certificates.

"Weren't you in three events?" was all he said. But he seemed pleased enough.

The three boys were all county sprinters and handy rugby players. The four girls were equally talented and took many prizes, but, as they got into their later teens, the mere signalling of sporting potential was quite sufficient: its fulfilment would have been considered a bit driven.

Increasingly, my sisters invested their time, as far as I could see, in endless tea-fuelled conversations around the kitchen table, usually with Mother chairing. If unobtrusive, I was sometimes permitted to attend. There I witnessed a clash of ideologies, like galaxies slowly colliding, linking arms and doing a highland fling.

A 1920s Irish Catholic rural conservative sensibility versus a burgeoning British feminism, secularism and egalitarianism. (Eilish read *Cosmopolitan* like an instruction manual. Still does. As I usually do when she's finished.)

But back in Northamptonshire, at least we lived in the country, and God made the country. We had a right of way over the fields, where we walked and talked endlessly. We must have been the only family in the village who walked simply for the joy of it: sometimes en masse, often in smaller denominations. In the cold winters, we walked many miles at a time.

In the summertime, too, but then we would also picnic by a stream and maybe paddle in the clear water and sink our feet into the fresh, deep-green cow muck that lay below. We would catch sticklebacks with nets bought at the newsagents and collect frogspawn in jam jars.

The sheep, though not ours, were reassuring reminders of the farm in Mayo and the cattle somehow echoed their Irish counterparts in Cork. Mostly Herefords and Friesians, their calves remain to my mind the most beautiful of creatures.

On a walk one day, I asked Father, almost as a querent, what would happen if birds became extinct?

He replied that that could never happen.

From that moment on, I knew he was fallible. Of course, it could happen. How couldn't he see that?

We could all become extinct: that much was apparent.

Another time, I told him that I would one day live, not in a house, but in a tunnel in a hill. He helpfully informed me that the place would need a good damp-course. Even though just a kid at the time, I found this an encouraging response.

I remember looking on once as he messed up a carpentry job on a door and muttered: I know it's a poor workman who blames his tools, but these really are useless tools—

I was sorry to see him berate himself. After a think, I concluded that just because a poor workman blames his tools, it doesn't follow that everyone who blames his tools is a bad workman. Introduction to basic logic.

Dad's dexterity could maybe be salvaged.

Being the youngest, I had a year alone with Mother before I went to school. She made her own bread, and took pleasure in my appetite for it. She talked to me as if I were a grown-up and seemed to find me a worthy audience. I was definitely regarded as a tad slow compared with my siblings but in a strangely fond way.

My treat was a few stalks of raw rhubarb with a saucer of sugar for dipping. I talked far too fast, and Mother would hold my arms by my side as she got me to repeat sentences slowly. She instilled in us all, competitiveness, spirit, disdain, wit and joy-in-outsider-ness. Although a professing Catholic, she's also a recognisably pre-Christian type, a member of the warrior caste and an enthusiastic exponent of conditional love. Naturally, I love her absolutely, in return.

In Shenington, old men would sit on the bench in the village square, talking about The Somme. Some of them had only ever left the village to go to war: no wonder they had a poor view of the wider world. Children's comics were called things like *Victor* or *Valiant* and were primers of xenophobia. German and Japanese troops still died daily on those pages, and richly deserved to.

(The first foreign words I learnt—apart from church Latin—were *schweinhund* and *banzai.* Barely enough to pass your way on a package holiday.)

For those of a more 3D inclination, bags of plastic soldiers could be bought for a few pence, in grey, blue, green and beige. All boys played with toy guns of one kind or another. A game without simulated killing was scarcely imaginable.

If children misbehaved in the street, adults would still shout: "I'll have you reported!"

But by then, no one knew to whom.

On most Sunday afternoons, John Wayne would assure us that American Indians deserved annihilation for not warmly welcoming invasion, infection and subjugation.

And that although women may have feigned resistance to an uninvited embrace, they would soon succumb and then be dizzily grateful. All duly noted.

The village schools had changed little since the Edwardian period: The Sixties must have been happening somewhere else. We were taught by three ageing spinsters in the Infants' School.

From my first day, I led a gang of four or five boys, two of them farmers' sons. I was naturally bossy and expected compliance, addressing them by surnames only. I would always try to spot Phillip Thurlow's mother at the school gate. She was a film-star beautiful, to me at least. Soon I would form an attachment to Lady Penelope, Marina (from

Stingray), Jeannie (from *Randall & Hopkirk*), Julie Christie, Mary Tyler Moore, Audrey Hepburn and Diana Rigg.

I'm just a normal bloke, after all. I'm not made of iron.

Infants' school smelled of crayons and milk. We painted murals and were awarded coloured stars for good work. We were rather brilliantly read to, and occasionally classical music was portentously played: the teachers examining our faces for the least flicker of appreciation.

The Junior School was a vast red brick pile opposite the Anglican church and only six doors up the street from our house. Boys and girls had separate playgrounds and generally sat apart, too. Desks were in rows and ink pots still in use. The teacher's desk was slightly raised on a dais. Windows were too high to offer distraction. At the front, under glass, were posters of plants, minerals and sponges, as well as a black-and-white photograph of Michelangelo's Pieta. We were very well taught.

Nonetheless, I regret being bashed around quite a bit by the headmaster, who was approaching retirement. I regret bashing others, too, even more.

In the playground, I was always prepared to settle disputes with my fists and found that victory granted various powers and rights. Once my mother found a victim of mine, a boy a year older than me and from a very deprived background, sitting on the school steps, his nose bleeding. She asked, who did this, Sam? Your son, he replied.

This led to an uncomfortable conversation on my arrival home that day. Sam was to die at sixteen in a motorbike accident. We hadn't spoken since the fight. Another time, my sisters told mother they had seen a stream of blood on the school steps on their way home from the convent. I did that to

Chalky, I said proudly, and was shocked to be execrated rather than carried around the room on a chair to a chorus of Yankee Doodle Dandy.

Had I miscalculated in some way?

On St Patrick's Day, we would each wear a small decorative harp and a sprig of shamrock, sent over from Mayo. The teacher would call me up to address the class about the (Welsh or English) patron saint of Ireland. The vigil on Croagh Patrick, slavery, druids, chieftains, snakes and miracles. I would look around the class menacingly. Anyone got a problem with any of this?

As if already aware that school wasn't up to much, in the greatest act of courage of my childhood, I approached Mother in the kitchen and asked her to buy me the weekly children's magazine, *Tell Me Why*. I was dumbstruck when she said yes, without too much persuasion. Asking for anything at all was not done.

When I was ten, I won a ten-shilling book token as a class prize. In the shop, I hovered for an age in front of a dull and dated ten-shilling book, stepping sideways every now and then to examine a big and colourful alternative a shelf away. This minuet was an obvious and intended plea for Father to add a few bob to my prize and buy the better book. But Dad stood silently behind me for a similar age and we left the shop with the ten-shilling book. The one I had earned and no more.

In the long school holidays, my brother Redmond (one year my senior) and I would play on our friends' farms. We suddenly had paddocks and stables, barns, playrooms and gardens to occupy us.

Best of all, in the attic of Robert Ashby's huge, wisteria-covered farmhouse, we found Swastika flags, Union Jacks, service rifles, shell cases and army helmets. Robert's father had been in the RAF and a Spitfire propeller with a clock as its centre straddled the chimneypiece.

We had boundless energy and gradually explored the village and then all the surrounding villages: Ashby St Ledger's, Great Brington, East Haddon, Yelvertoft, Crick, Weedon, Little Brington, Fawsley, Ravensthorpe, West Haddon—

Perhaps improbably, we looked inside the churches, drew maps, made sketches (there are Lutyens cottages in Ashby) and bought oven-hot buns from the bakery in East Haddon.

I suppose we also noted the pub signs for future reference.

At eleven, Tommy Knowles, Robert Ashby and Philip Thurlow all went off to an independent boarding school. I saw little of them again. The lost generation. Tommy died last year, just before his eighteenth birthday. Another motorbike casualty.

***

Church was a decisive social divide. Most people were non-Catholic.

In fact, most were non-anything. Even those who attended the Anglican St Etheldreda's church opposite our house seemed a bit lukewarm and almost exclusively middle class, unlike the wider mix of our church, where Norman St John-Stevas would occasionally visit from Fawsley and sit next to families from the council houses.

Being a Catholic wasn't a small thing. It was intense, imbuing every subject with meaning. And it was Manichaean, dividing everything into good and bad, light and dark, in a taxonomy no outsider would ever fully grasp. We attended not the beautiful pre-Reformation church across the street, but the navvy-built hut at the very opposite end of the village.

We would walk there feeling tired and hungry (no food being permitted before communion) and take up a couple of pews on the left. The women at the back would gossip loudly until the first words of Mass were uttered, by a priest who was usually Scots or Irish, though some were English toffs and one a Dutch intellectual.

Clouds of incense filled the air and incantatory Latin united and transported the congregation. We were now part of the billion worldwide Catholics, even the communion of saints, and no longer a minority village sect. We would sing *Sweet Sacrament Divine* and listen to very uneven sermons, one or two concerning the Cheltenham races, others the pre-conversion pride of St Augustine of Hippo.

(Who, like The Buddha, was a runaway dad: a fact not much stressed in sermons.)

The priest would come to our house afterwards for coffee and toast (and a smoke) before driving to Yelvertoft to say Mass there. Mum would laugh strenuously at poor jokes. Dad would initiate theological debate – bit too early in the day, perhaps.

All three of us were altar boys. And all the children attended weekly catechism, which was at that time (Vatican II) changing from the old Q and A format to something resembling a seminar. So we would sit for an hour with a priest discussing sin, charity, faith, the Trinity, parables, the Atonement (even then, of dubious coherence to me) and good versus evil. We also saw colour slides of the Holy Land, which made us feel rather cosmopolitan.

I remember walking home from catechism with Redmond (we must have been nine and ten) when a boy a little older than us, Andrew Chambers, jauntily crossed the road from his house to intercept us. He was beaming. His father stood at the gate, proudly looking on. In his high-pitched voice, Andrew asked us how a man could be in some bread and enquired, glancing back at his sponsoring father, if we were cannibals.

I suspect the finer points of transubstantiation might have been wasted on him, even if we had them to hand. But I remember the rage I felt. This was around the same time the Reverend Ian Paisley was in the newspapers after holding up a stolen communion wafer at the Oxford Union, where he made the audience gasp and grin as he mockingly waved it around.

But how anyone could see bread without also seeing the meaning of bread?

Could anyone look at a word or a picture without also looking beyond it?

Could you look at a fellow creature and not sense a secret, invisible, self within?

Isn't all of life about appearances and the need to delve beneath and beyond them?

And in my own body, wasn't bread turned daily into flesh?

Surely the world was not what you saw with your eyes, but what you grasped with your mind. And your mind was your history, your poetry, your family and your dreams.

Only idiots saw just with their eyes.

I certainly said none of this at the time.

But I inarticulately felt something very like it.

***

Mum and Dad dislike it when we say our upbringing was unusual in any way. But we talk about it amongst ourselves (the kids, that is) all the time.

It's hard to know what their policy was, if they had one. But if it was full integration they were after, they went about it very strangely.

Not just the indomitable Irishry. The Catholic thing too.

Just recently I've been thinking about this for the first time.

The two of them are really adherents of completely different religions.

What Mum likes about the church is hierarchy. Exclusivity. Theatre. Rules. Hardship. Superiority. Glamour. Inflexibility. Even the misogyny. And the possibility of eternal damnation, of course. She likes the form of religion but isn't very interested in the content. I think if everyone were Catholic, it would lose some of its appeal for Mum. Being in a minority is somehow vital to her.

(During the War, Mum nursed Violet Gibson in a private mental hospital. She was the Irishwoman who was sectioned after she shot Mussolini in the nose. Mum and Violet got on quite well. On a bad day, I wonder if they may have even swapped identities.)

With Dad, it couldn't be more different. He doesn't care for any of those showy religious things one bit. He probably thinks they're ludicrous. It's the content that matters to him, not the form. He thinks we should look after the worst-off and be careful not to envy the better-off. That's the whole of his gospel. That's why he's always sitting on committees, organising parties for old people and raising money for the St Vincent de Paul Society.

She's a Druid and he's a Stoic. Christianity hardly comes into it.

Maybe if they do return to Ireland, they'll fit right in. Who knows?

But some people say there's no going back.

You can't step into the same river twice.

(They won't leave a kitty when they go. It just wouldn't occur. I think we all turned eighteen the day Dad had his heart attack.)

***

3
Folsom Prison Blues

I spent last week in Brighton. My summer holiday before the factory swallows me up.

Sheelagh invited me down. She's a student there. French and German. It's the fag-end of hippie culture; the town's psychedelic and yet still seedy and post-war. She kitted me out in a fisherman's smock, velvet loons and clogs—the uniform of the University of Sussex students, apparently. I don't think I'll wear them around Shenington somehow. Still, it's nice being someone's project for a day or two.

The shops in Brighton are full of Art Nouveau mirrors and Mucha posters; the record shops smell of patchouli. We ate at Leadbelly's and walked around The Lanes.

Sheelagh's northern friend, Marianne, politely affected an interest in the book I was reading, on Dadaism. I politely affected no interest in her legs.

Life was sweet last week.

And Sheelagh's a hoot.

But at the station, just as I was leaving, she told me she'd been diagnosed with multiple sclerosis. Look it up, she said, as the train pulled out.

Ferguson's hasn't changed since last year. Why would it? I work mostly on lathes, turning, drilling and reaming parts. It's boring me to death.

(See what I did there?)

The factory floor is huge and deafening. The full-timers look as if Johnny Cash had just cancelled on them. Everything is grey and metallic. Even the air is full of tiny silver specks. (Don't inhale.)

The full-timers openly resent the summer workforce. We can leave in September after all. And we don't pay tax. And we read in our breaktimes. And we laugh among ourselves. They don't.

We are not lifers: not serious.

Today, a young woman is being marched around, steered by a group of older women. She's been wrapped in a paper dress and headdress, cut and stapled in the packing room. All the women coo, a sound that can be heard over the chattering machines. She is to be married this weekend. Her husband-to-be, Trev, is working here too: grinning as he looks on, like an extra from *Deliverance*.

(I don't think he could count to eleven without taking a shoe off.)

They can't be more than seventeen or eighteen. My age.

Why coo? Sadism, I suppose.

What chance do they have? It looks like a Minoan sacrifice.

And everyone coos.

Sometimes, I have to climb on the bench to fix the compressed air pipe above my head. Then it's my turn to hear the women coo, as my T-shirt rides up and they can see my bare belly. Some of the machines are covered in pornography, personalised by the women, now in Spain on holiday, who usually work there.

(Two days ago, I was cooed relentlessly and didn't know why. After a while, a forewoman came up to me and removed the porn photo someone had stuck on my back without my knowing. I was scarlet. More cooing: much more.)

By 10 o'clock every morning, I've had enough. It's impossible not to look at your watch a hundred times before the siren goes off at five. Only the weekends make it possible.

A chance to do something you can regret all the next week. That seems to be the approved system, anyway.

***

4
Fête

It's Saturday morning and I'm tired and aching. At least, the sun is shining and decorates my bedroom wall. It was great not having to get up at half-six.

It's not as hot as last year, but it's still a pellucid summer and people are wearing bright clothes and talking more loudly than they usually do. Radio One plays The Eagles endlessly. *Hotel California. Take it Easy.* Oh and Hot Chocolate. (Which is not good.)

They keep going on about The Jubilee. Oh God. Just, Oh God.

I need toast.

At least, I don't have to shave anymore and can grow a beard. I'll keep it cropped close. Don't want to look like a folk singer.

At mid-morning, I walk rather half-heartedly up the shady rhododendron pathway to the vicarage, where the village fête is being held. (Well, it's a change of scenery. And practically everyone goes.) There are all the traditional things: tombola, bale-throwing, a brass band, cakes, vegetable and watercolour competitions, children's entertainers. A few vintage cars.

Stanley Unwin, who lives in the village, gives a speech which is deliberately incomprehensible. It's genuinely funny because he delivers it deadpan. His face is impassive and his arms flail as he patiently explains himself in an idiolect no one will ever understand. Half the people in the audience are wreathed in smiles and the other half simply don't get the joke—which adds something. Speech was given to man so he could disguise his thoughts. I read that somewhere.

After a while, the vicar's wife, Mrs Courtney, beckons me over. She is smiling and talking animatedly to another woman who is holding the handlebars of her old-fashioned sit-up-and-beg.

Mrs Courtney looks exactly as a vicar's wife should: hair pinned back by tortoiseshell slides, Fair Isle cardigan, glasses, ankle socks, tweed skirt, flat brown brogues.

"Fergus, I want you to meet Elodie. She's French and she's interested in philosophy. Elodie, Fergus has just finished at school and his sister Aisleen tells me he's off to study philosophy this autumn."

Elodie proffers her hand (which I don't expect) and we shake. She's wearing a Paddington hat and sunglasses.

I soon gather that she lives in the next village, East Haddon. I don't venture any of my French. Too risky. She is confident and smiling. Her English is perfect. She asks me where I hope to study and I say, University College London.

"And who is your favourite thinker?"

I'm not ready for this.

"Plato. Or maybe Sartre." (*Oh Christ.*)

She smiles benignly. (Or maybe matronisingly.)

"And you, you've studied philosophy?" I enquire.

"Yes, of course. We had to. In France, we do theory of knowledge for the Bacc. But I also elected to do the philosophy paper and even spent a year at university doing philosophy—before I dropped out, that is."

She smiles. (Is dropping out an achievement of some sort?)

Mrs Courtney excuses herself and moves away to greet some newcomers.

Elodie asks me how I plan to spend the summer and I (hilariously) describe life at Ferguson's. She wonders if I would be interested in working for her for a few weeks. She will be selling-up soon. She has to. The house is practically empty, but the whole interior needs painting. Stables too. And the garden needs work; the trees and the herb borders are out of control. And there is a small kitchen garden going to ruin.

I lamely comment that I should be able to paint as I did Art A-Level. Zero response.

(I have actually done loads of decorating. Mostly in Eilish's place, but I don't say so for some reason.)

I add that I have worked as a gardener before, in the old people's home, Boar's Hill, halfway between East Haddon and here.

She smiles and says, "Well, then."

After a brief chat about payment, I say yes. And thank you.

(I've had enough of the factory and this feels like a liberation. And I think I can live with the pay cut.)

"I'll be there on Monday. Chard House. First house on the right as I enter the village. Eight?"

"God no. Nine or ten will be fine."

***

5
Chard House

It's five to nine as I cycle up the gravel drive, which is lined with lime trees.

As it levels out, I see Chard House, which is sandstone and facing the entrance, a two-pillared stone portico at its front. To my right is a red brick courtyard and what look like stables. The drive seems to continue to the lawn behind the house. It has a cedar tree at its centre and the grass around it is like hessian. Beyond that is a high brick wall covered in wisteria.

I park my bike by the crimson front door and lift and release the heavy knocker, which is a black iron lion's paw.

After a few moments, the door opens and Elodie comes out to meet me.

She's relaxed and smiling and dressed in a white skirt, white cheesecloth shirt and espadrilles. She says she's about to make coffee but may as well show me around first. She glances at my bike.

First, she leads me to the stable block. It's messy and the walls need whitewashing. As we turn back to the house, she gestures to the left and says the limes need cutting back. They are usually pollarded, but not this year. Then we go right and

I see the long lean-to garden shed with rusty corrugated roofing.

"Everything you need is in there, I hope," she says.

As we walk along, I look inside, a lawn mower, saws, secateurs, weed killer, paint, whitewash, brushes, hoes, rakes, forks, spades—

We look beyond the high wall to the kitchen garden, which has more or less gone wild.

She waves a hand at it and looks away in dismay.

"Anything you can do there. Anything!"

We go back to the house and into the kitchen, where Elodie fills the kettle and flicks it on. A cafetière is standing ready and a tin of ground coffee stands already opened.

The kitchen is big, high-ceilinged and almost empty. It must freeze in winter but is pleasantly cool today. On one wall is a huge sideboard with empty plate racks and brass drawer-handles.

There are a few cardboard boxes on the grey stone floor and there is some post on the pine table, which is flanked by only two chairs, one with arms.

We can go round the house in a minute, she says, as she spoons-in the coffee and pours in the steaming water.

We sit. The coffee is strong and delicious and black. We both have huge cups that need both hands.

"I can make toast!" She gestures airily to a bread bin.

"No thanks, I'm fine."

Elodie is quite talkative and seems so at ease with the world. Amused even. She's certainly no slave-driver, I suspect.

She explains that she will come and go. Rather busy. I must ask if unsure about anything. Break as often as I need.

Maybe bring my own lunch. Or try The Wheatsheaf in the village. They do rolls. But there will be food here too. Finish around five or half-five?

Then she says, "Oh yes. Tell me about your time at Boar's Hill. You said you'd done some work there."

Oh God, I think. I hope she doesn't expect a proper gardener. (Or painter.)

Well, I say. I was only sixteen at the time—

I start to remember Boar's Hill out loud; try to conjure it up without exposing my inexpertise too much.

As I speak, for the first time, I start to carefully look at her.

She's quite old. Mid-thirties or so. But I can't help noticing that she's still attractive. Tanned. Green eyes. No make-up. Dark hair, tied back. A bit skinny maybe. But womanly. Confident. And most of all, she seems to treat me like an equal. Or something like it.

She listens very attentively. More than I'm used to.

"Well, two years ago, my brother Redmond and I spent most of the summer working there. We dug, cut, mowed, weeded and trimmed. Retrieved the rockery…We used to have lunch with the more demented of the residents, Ivy, Rose and Mabel. Mabel would sometimes make a break for the gates, eighty metres up the straight driveway. She wasn't a fast walker and I could give her a twenty minutes start, then get in the dumper truck, overtake her and gently turn her round. Then she would, almost involuntarily, walk all the way back. She called me a black devil. I suppose because of my hair. I didn't contradict her, I'm afraid. She used to tie her belt around her head. Maybe she'd been a flapper…"

Elodie nods very seriously, and says:

"So, a little deranged then—"

I decide to go on.

"Once I was up a ladder, trimming the top of a huge yew hedge with electric cutters, when I noticed an old lady at the foot of the ladder, calling up to me. So I took off my ear protectors, but I still couldn't hear her. (I'm miming now.) I put them down and the cutters, took off my gloves, carefully came down the ladder and asked if I could be of help. And she said, "Cutting the hedge, are you?""

I smile as I finish this little sketch, but Elodie is looking even more serious. Concerned even.

"Very lonely, I expect," she says.

My smile fades.

One more try.

"Another time, just before we left, a very old man and his deckchair toppled sideways on the gravel. His head was quite bashed in. Redmond and I got him back into his seat and called the nurse. We noticed that as she cleaned the wound, he took the chance to—stroke her breasts. Redmond and I were rather impressed by his—"

"Presence of mind?" She suggests, frowning slightly.

"Yes, I suppose," I say weakly.

(Wish I hadn't told that one. *Arse.*)

Elodie suddenly looks business-like and pushes her chair back.

We drain our coffee cups and leave them on the table.

"Let's look over the house. Then I must be off into town," she says.

We quickly go through all the rooms. She wasn't kidding about it being empty. One sofa and a coffee table in the living room and a tiny transistor radio. All the furniture and carpets have been removed. On the wall, a Balthus exhibition poster of a woman in a kimono, sitting on a chair.

We stand in the doorway of Elodie's bedroom. It looks lived-in, but even here the floorboards are bare, except for a really ugly orange and brown rug, of abstract intent. The mattress is on the floor, but the bed neatly made. There is an old walnut wardrobe and a Bang and Olufsen hi-fi.

I ask if I can look at her (very few) LPs and she seems not to mind; Georges Moustaki (?), Ella Fitzgerald, Nat King Cole, Leonard Cohen, Carole King, Brahms' Intermezzi (?), Gerald Finzi (?).

Slightly wiser by now, I decide not to comment.

There is a tall pile of Jean Plaidy paperbacks in the corner and another exhibition poster on the wall. (Vuillard.)

Above the marble mantelpiece is a mirror, fitted all the way up to the high ceiling and on the shelf itself, a green leather travel clock, a postcard of a Morandi painting of jugs and a bizarre marble statuette.

We go downstairs and she briefly explains which order to emulsion the rooms in. All whites and greys.

Then she leaves, and moments later I hear her car tootling down the lane.

***

6
Elodie

I've been here for a week now. Mostly just getting on with it by myself.

Working steadily. Not too fast, not too slow. When it's fine, I work in the garden, cutting-back mostly and trying to retrieve the vegetable garden. When it's raining, I work indoors, either in the house or the stables, painting the walls and some of the woodwork. I'm keen to do a good job. I'm grateful I've escaped the factory. Redemption. Salvation. Exuviation.

The outer garden has some incredible trees. Copper beech. Horse chestnut. Black walnut. They all have immense personalities. You can't help feeling they're trying to say something we need to hear. Gently waving their arms. Looking more dignified than us. I told Elodie yesterday how much I love them and why.

Elodie usually leaves food in the kitchen and tells me to help myself.

Quiche, cheese, roll-mop herrings, paté, cold veal, tapenade—

It took her a couple of days to realise I don't eat any of these things.

I select some bread, some potato salad, some boiled eggs.

"Were you brought up by an elevator?" she asks, not realising how mortified I am by my inability to eat more than a few kinds of food.

***

At four, Elodie's dark blue Fiat 128 crunches up the drive in a cloud of dust. She waves and smiles and takes her shopping into the house.

After a short while, she walks onto the lawn with a glass of white wine in one hand and a stubby bottle of French blond beer in the other and places them on the round garden table.

She sits on one of the white wrought-iron chairs and puts her feet up on another.

"Come on over," she calls. "That's enough for one week."

By the time I join her after a quick cold wash, she's lit-up. Silk Cut.

She pushes the beer towards me and I say thanks.

Elodie has put on a Georges Moustaki record (*Here's to You*) and left her bedroom window open so we can hear it in the garden.

She's wearing a powder blue summer dress and white sandals.

"Weren't we going to talk philosophy at some point? What are you reading?" she asks.

I tell her about my reading list. *Euthyphro. Phaedrus. Utilitarianism. Meditations.* As I have all these in second-hand paperbacks, I'm starting with them.

Elodie seems satisfied with this. She's thinking. But before she can respond, I say, "Do you mind my asking? How did you get to end up here, in East Haddon? In this house?"

She takes a drag and narrows her eyes.

"Ah yes. My story. Of course. I can tell you. You know I am French, yes? I grew up near Compiègne, in the countryside. Our farm is called La Chesnaie. It's rather large by English standards. Dozens of combine harvesters. Lots of smaller farms on the estate. Father seldom leaves the place, and runs it with my younger brother, Thierry. Mother died not long ago." (I frown a little.)

"Anyway, I was sent away to a private school until I was sixteen. Holidays in Cavalaire. Skiing at Chamonix. All very nice. But then I insisted I should be allowed to go to the local state school—Lycée Henry IV. That's where I got interested in philosophy, I suppose. But I'm not answering your question, am I? At La Chesnaie, we loved show jumping. We competed all over northern France, Germany, Switzerland, Belgium. When I was nineteen, I met an Englishman who was representing the British Army. He was forty-one. He took one look at me and said I was exactly his type. I suppose I was flattered. We simply fell in love and got married and I moved here. Henry Fleetwood. This was his home."

"And your family was OK with that?"

"Not in an absolute sense, no. But I didn't mind. I just left and didn't look back. Very French. I'm here now forever. I shan't return. I've learnt to love England and the British, and it suits me."

"So, where is your husband now?"

"Of course, you don't know. He died two years ago in Northern Ireland. It wasn't a violent death, if that's what you're thinking. He had a heart attack and was gone. Since then it's all been probate, taxes, wills, selling our horses—now the house. We had twelve years together and now it's over. Now, I am my own mistress."

"And so what comes next, Elodie?"

She smiles ruefully and stubs out her cigarette.

"I have very little money. I also need very little and want very little. I'm rich in that sense. If I need to ride out, I can always hire a horse somewhere. I hope to move to Yorkshire and rent a small place and start over again. It's really that simple."

After a short lull, she says, "So tell me about this utilitarianism. I don't really know that one. Then another time tell me about one of those dialogues you mentioned."

"Well, OK. Very roughly, Mill thinks we've got it all wrong. Totally. We're concerned with right and wrong but hopeless at understanding it. Like a child trying maths that's way beyond them. We use our traditions and our feelings to work things out. And the law. Which is a big mess. And of course, religion. Big mess too. And instinct about what seems natural. Yet another big mess. They're all wrong."

"So, what does he suggest?"

"He seems to think there's a true measure that we can discover through philosophy. We can calculate what will bring about the greatest happiness of the greatest number. It's all very fair and terribly British." (I do the accent. *Stupid*.) "There must be a factual amount that we can maximise. We're sentient. Things make us happy or sad. And it's not just humans. It's all sentient creatures that count. So instead of bothering with Stone Age documents like the Old Testament, we should start from scratch and work it all out. Women.

Homosexuality. Marriage. Education. Animals. The environment. Our attitude to all these things should change."

"So, maybe, we should do as we are told by his big computer, no? The Old French would love that. An enlightened despot. But I don't think the Young French would allow it. Onto the streets!" She smiles, and continues,

"So we are sitting here drinking and we should be cooking and cleaning for old people. Is that it?"

"Maybe we should. A lot of people would need to give up a lot for the overall happiness level to rise. But most would gain. That's the point." (I'm sounding too earnest.)

"You know our old President, de Gaulle, he said happiness is for idiots."

This stops me in my tracks.

"So what then? What do we actually want, Elodie?"

"Maybe reality. With all its ups and downs. Maybe we don't really want happiness: we just say we do. Like sanctity." (*God, she's French.*) "Which we run from," she adds.

"Fergus, if you could go now into a dream for the rest of your life and be perfectly happy, would you do that?"

"I'm not sure. I hate drugs and that sounds pretty druggy. I suppose I'm curious about how things will turn out in this life."

"So, reality is a value for you, then?"

"Yes. I think it is. If you can find it. I'm not sure—"

"Your friend Mill—sounds like someone hurt him really badly. That's what I think."

She sips her wine and looks into the middle-distance.

***

7
Symposium

It's Monday evening and I've put in a good shift.

It's cooler today and will rain tonight, I'm pretty sure.

I hear Elodie opening her bedroom window and then Georges Moustaki.

A few minutes later, she appears in the garden and sits on her chair with her legs lying flat across another. Madame Récamier. She's wearing a colourful shawl and hugging herself, as if freezing. No drinks this time. (Not a Friday.)

After chatting over the day together, she says she's been thinking about Mill.

She's keen to say she's all for better conditions for women and animals and so on, but she's unwilling to give up her freedom that easily and she's sure that's the inevitable outcome of his philosophy. If we're told how to live our lives, they'd hardly be our lives, would they?

Elodie says it might be fine for social policy, this principle. But in her personal life, she doesn't even try to stick to rules.

"So, how do you make decisions then, assuming you believe in right and wrong?" I ask.

"I certainly do believe," she says, slightly indignantly.

"I'm simply saying there aren't any rules. This is what the poets know and the philosophers don't. Look at paintings. No one says a painting must have lots of blue. Or a yellow vase. Or a woman's back. We just see individual good paintings. They're all quite unalike. All they have in common is that they're good. I find life very—specific, if you like. We are asked to be connoisseurs of every new day."

She looks at me sideways and lights up a Silk Cut.

"So, tell me about one of those dialogues. You choose."

"Well, OK, Elodie. But I've really only skimmed them. Let's skip the *Euthyphro* because we're liable to agree. But it's a good example of the elenchus. Dialogue. Swapping ideas and testing them. But you probably know much more about Plato than I do. You must have studied him in France…"

Looking more animated, she says, "That might be true, but it's a little while ago now. At school, we studied the *Gorgias* and the *Republic*. Plato thought we were born with buried memories, and when we experience the world, it can jog those memories, if you are a philosopher, that is. I remember thinking it must be like an identity parade: I can't remember the face of my burglar well enough to do a photo-fit, but when I see him, I certainly recognise him! My crazy witch of a teacher said that without these ancient memories, we would be like a dog in a library: able to see colours and shapes, but not able to see books and labels. That requires a little more. So if I ask you Fergus, what justice is, you will probably be silent. But if I pay you this week, you will recognise it as a just act. Unlike a dog who might be watching!" She laughs.

"That all sounds good to me," I say. "Wish I'd had your teacher, by the way. I've only just started the *Phaedrus*, which is a bit weirder. You may know it. Socrates is keeping cool by a stream outside the city walls and Phaedrus appears and says he's just heard a great lecture by Lysias. Socrates doesn't seem to like the countryside and says you can't learn anything from trees. (He may be wrong about that.) But anyway, Phaedrus more or less recites the lecture, which was apparently pretty scandalous. Lysias argued that a relationship should be a deal. A cool, rational transaction. Not the result of the kind of craziness that lovers so often go in for. He thinks it's better all round. Something like that."

Elodie interjects, "Well, maybe Lysias or whoever, has a point. I was brought up believing in romantic love. Most people are. Here in the West anyway. My friends and I *longed* to lose our minds! That was everything to us! And every movie we saw, or book we read, told us that if it didn't happen, our lives were a waste. We'd be dried up."

"But then it happened to you too, didn't it?" I ask.

Elodie pauses for a long time. She's practically doing a mime of weighing me up.

"In France we say *coup de foudre*. That's a real thing. Yes, that happened to me. And it can cost you, you know. But you don't care because it's the only thing that matters. The only thing. My best friends asked me what I saw in Henry. No one would put us two together. And I couldn't tell them. I thought that was a good thing. A symptom of true love. I couldn't point to one thing—his looks, his manner, his mind. I just adored him and really almost betrayed myself and everything

I had for him. I did it willingly and joyfully. I thought my friends idiots. I felt sorry for them. But now, of course, looking back, I'm allowed to wonder. Maybe it was the smell of hay or the sweat of those beautiful horses. Perhaps it was the weather on that day we met. Or his riding boots!"

After a lull I say, rather conventionally, "But you were happy, weren't you?"

Elodie looks at me directly.
"Even a happy drunk is a drunk, Fergus," she murmurs.
"An addict in a garden of poppies is still an addict. In a play, when someone is poisoned with a love potion, it's a cause for laughter. Comedy. But in real life it's not like that, I think. Your soul is occupied by a foreign power. You are suddenly like France in The War. You are asked to collude with your captor. And to smile doing it. Which you do willingly, because your will has been—anaesthetised."

"But in the *Symposium*—famously—Socrates says that falling in love is like joining your other half," I say.

Elodie looks unimpressed and slightly angry as she replies, "So maybe his mathematics was not that good after all. It's more like being halved than doubled. For some, anyway. Maybe for most. For most women."

I say, "But Socrates goes on later to defend ecstatic love as divine. He rebukes Lysias for being so cheap and calculating."

"That's all very fine, I'm sure," she replies, "But how do you know which is which? How can you tell if it's divine or just insane? Didn't Socrates himself fall in love with the appalling Alcibiades? He's one to talk! Most people—most women maybe—after the potion wears off a little, they start to discover their lover's true qualities. But I think they should start there—with their qualities, I mean. If that's what Lysias means, then I agree with him. Good for Lysias. Since my husband died, I have found out much more about him than I ever knew when he was alive. And it's only now that I know him…Did you notice that statuette in my bedroom, Fergus?"

"Not really," I reply. "Not closely, I mean." (*Damn.*)

"I bought it when my mother died, with some money she left me. It's French, of course. Eighteenth Century. *Venus Chastising Cupid*. It's the first thing I look at every morning."

After some time, Elodie looks at me and tells me she's usually very private. I'm a surprisingly good listener, for a man.

I say, "It must be due to having so many sisters. I like listening to them."

Then she says, "Oh, sisters, of course," and laughs out loud, as if at a private joke.

"Now, you know about me. So tell me about you."

And I do. At length.

One version, selected from many.

***

8
The Roads to Freedom

"You said Sartre."

"I beg your pardon, Elodie?"

It's Friday and this time we're both drinking wine on the lawn.

Elodie is wearing a big dark blue cardigan over her white tennis kit and she's kicked off her plimsolls. She played with friends in the village earlier. Her hair is in a thick plait, tied with a navy ribbon.

"At the fête. You said you like Sartre."

(She sounds a bit accusatory, as she can.)

"Well, I don't know that much about him, really. It's the idea of radical freedom that appeals. That in every situation we have choices. We shouldn't be shaped just by our backgrounds, or by convention. That would be totally arbitrary. We're so much more free than we like to admit. Freedom is intimidating. So we pretend we're not very free. We go along with expectations and with what has gone before. We live second-hand lives. We don't think afresh, for ourselves. I think that's all true. I see it everywhere. And I don't really want it to happen to me."

(As I say this, I suddenly feel more juvenile than I like.)

Elodie smiles and looks around.

"So you see it everywhere? But people see green grass everywhere and grass isn't green, is it? It only looks green because of our eyes and brains interpret it that way. Saying you see something everywhere isn't evidence. You may be like the paranoid man who sees people following him—everywhere!"

I pause to have a think. (Maybe she should go first.)

"So what do you think, Elodie? I won't ask what you see *everywhere*—"

"Well, today—in this conversation at least—I don't think there's much freedom at all. Maybe none. Yes, our backgrounds, nationalities, religions, sex, all these things matter, whether we like it or not. Would you like Sartre's ideas if you hadn't actually come across his work? Everything you have told me about yourself tells me why you are the way you are. You know that yourself. But other things, too. Could you change your mind for me now? It's *your mind* after all, Fergus."

"Well, I suppose I could. But I'd prefer not to."

"Exactly. You can't then. Please believe the world is flat. For me. Now!"

(She giggles. Is it the wine or me looking stupid? Or both, of course.)

"You know I can't do that. That's—not possible," I admit.

"And so it goes for all your beliefs," she adds triumphantly, "They have you, you don't have them! They live inside your head, doing their thing. Like bees in a beehive."

(She may be a tiny bit squiffy.)

"People say they've changed their mind, but they never do. Newspapers do! Friends do! Statistics do!" she adds.

"But I do sometimes change my mind, Elodie. I go on a walk and think and I change my mind about things."

"That's not you doing it. That's *your reason* doing it. You think things through and you improve your opinion. And then you're stuck with it again. But listen, Fergus. This bit's important, I think. Being constrained by that kind of thinking *is being free*. A really free person may have absolutely no choice, whereas an idiot may choose to believe the moon is made of Brie or camels can speak French, or a million other things. But having all those options would make you insane, not free. And freedom is the very opposite. Freedom is the highest form of sanity. But it must be earned. No one is born free. Freedom means knowing and understanding and acting for a good reason. In Sartre, in *Les Chemins de la Liberté*, Matthieu stabs his hand precisely because there is no rational reason to and he thinks that makes him free! It's mad. Vraiment fou! I know an American here in the village. Lauren. She tells me how much choice she has in the shops there and how in America you can do whatever you want. The only free country! But I don't want that kind of choice. I want to be free *from it*. And I don't want to do just what I want. I want to want what I *should* want. Which can mean in truth that on all the big things, I have very few options. I'm Catholic, but I see what Luther meant when he said he could do no other. He was at his freest then, perhaps."

(I'm having embarrassing flashbacks of recent conversations when I may have been disastrously wrong.)

"But what if I just know I'm free? If I just sense it?"

"Then you *feel* free. It doesn't mean you *are*. I feel I'm a good tennis player, but sadly, the facts are against me…And another thing. Laplace said if we knew all the laws of physics and where every particle was at a particular point, he'd be able to predict everything in the future. Things only happen because they're caused, Fergus. Nothing just happens."

"But what if they did, Elodie?"

"Well, then we're back to Matthieu! We're crazy people who aren't answerable for what we do. In fact, we wouldn't really be *doing* anything. Things would just keep happening to us."

There's a long lull and Elodie pours more Sancerre and lights up.

I really get the impression she's thinking this out for the first time and I just happen to be here.

She continues, "So, I suppose, love and freedom are not so different—You can have rubbish versions and real versions. But we are mostly offered the rubbish ones: Hollywood; Sartre.

We need to know and understand and have rational control and do what's right.

Otherwise, we're junkies, or else robots who think they're free because they can buy what advertisements tell them to."

She glances at me and smiles, now her lovely, calm self again.

"This lesson was learnt the hard way, Fergus. Take note. If you love someone for a good reason instead of just infatuation, count yourself lucky. That way, if you have no choice about who you love, it's not such a catastrophe. It's more like being stuck with the fact the Earth is round. Which doesn't seem to bother you that much…"

9
Fatted Calf

Soon after I get in from work, Redmond walks in, drops a Tesco shopping bag full of books on the floor and slumps down.

"Hi, Bro. Sorry I didn't phone. Just need to pick up a few things." He hunches over, rolling a fag. Liquorice paper.

I make us both a cup of tea and join him.

He looks thinner than usual and even more like Keats, but with an earring. His knuckles are bruised and there are notes in biro on both hands.

He's wearing an old bum-freezer with small lapels, white shirt, drainpipe jeans and scuffed white plimsolls. His spiky hair reminds me that he's become a follower of the punk craze down in London. The anger and disillusionment they emit will suit him. Maybe he's found his tribe.

Later, in The Peacock (the Greaser pub) we sit in the corner and try to reconnect.

Sounds like he spends most of his time in Soho, at The Marquee.

(The Damned. The Stranglers. Patti Smith. The Ramones. The Sex Pistols...)

He writes reviews for the *NME* and *Time Out*, some in praise of punk: many more just disparaging heavy metal, glam rock and easy listening.

He's a critic in both senses. Big time.

When we get round to me, there's not much to say, I say.

We talk about Mum and Dad, maybe moving back to Ireland.

He's pretty unimpressed with the idea but says he's indifferent.

I try an observation about what's happening in Northern Ireland.

"Listen, mate. I don't want to hear this shit. I don't care about Ireland or nationalism or who's killing who or fucking why. OK? They're all a fucking shower and a disgrace. I get enough of this shit in Kilburn. Passing fucking tins around in pubs. I told them where they could shove them. Fucking tinkers."

We pause to let this moment pass.

People glance over from the pool table.

He's loud. His dog bites.

(Redmond combines a high moral tone with sweeping callousness. He's callous because he's so sensitive. Maybe.)

After a while, I say, I've been reading a bit of Yeats, falsely and ingratiatingly adding that his poetry was probably more like scripture to us than the Bible.

I immediately regret it.

He looks up from the spot on the floor that was seemingly annoying him and turns to me as if to study me for the first time.

"You're beginning to look like Nick Drake, mate. And sound like him."

(He's counting on his fingers now, his prosecution complex kicking in.)

"Sean didn't read Yeats. Mum and Dad didn't. The girls just read that Pre-Raphaelite shit. Only you and I read the later stuff. And no one knows what that's about, do they? Not a place called Ireland, that's for sure. I tell you it really *nauseates* me that he's always labelled Anglo-Irish or Protestant. He was an occultist, for Christ's sake. He hated Christianity. And he didn't come from anywhere or belong anywhere. In any way. That's the whole fucking point. He had a weird dream and was bonkers enough to go and live in it. Reality was just a bad trip for him. He's the crazy bloke sitting alone on the night bus, talking to himself with his hands in his mac pockets."

He calms down, slightly, and mutters;

"Move on, Chumbo. Try Shelley for Christ's sake. But please spare me."

His gaze returns to the floor. It must look less annoying than before.

I decide not to tell him about Elodie or where I'm working, and he doesn't ask.

He waves a finger as he orders himself another Pernod. Just the one.

Then a Queen track (*We are the Champions*) comes on the jukebox.

"Christ," he says, sitting up and looking around. "Which cunt put this on?"

10
Devil in the Flesh

On Monday night as I left, Elodie said she had something for me.

She handed me a small, newish, Penguin paperback. I was struck by the beautiful cover. A drawing (maybe in charcoal?) of a young man who looks directly at the viewer, with a faintly arrogant expression.

The book is called *Devil in the Flesh*, by Raymond Radiguet.

She told me she'd found it in the village second-hand bookshop.

Apparently, it was once a big deal.

Now, it's Thursday morning and we are having a fresh coffee while the rain pours down outside. There are already deep grey puddles on the gravel.

I've pulled my jersey on for the first time in days. The kitchen is dark.

She asks me if I've finished it yet and I say yes. (It's a tiny book after all.)

I tell her I wonder why she gave it to me. I really hated it.

(The young man—only a boy, in fact—who narrates the story, has an affair with a young woman, Marthe, whose husband is away fighting in the First World War.)

I can't hold back.

"He's a complete stoat. Full of shit and lies and deceit. He witters on about love and it's all utter crap. It's all a game to him. He doesn't even do lust properly. He just experiments with other people's lives. He seems to hate everyone. And his own feelings come across as totally false. He's a fraud. When he gets Marthe pregnant, he forbids her—forbids her—from going swimming! He wants her to kill herself. That would make him into a big man…"

Elodie touches my arm and says I seem quite upset. And she's right.

(I think I feel a bit insulted, but don't say so.)

I continue, perhaps less vehemently.

"Why on earth would I want to spend the last couple of evenings with a complete shit like him. And do as he wanted, peer into his empty life. It's as if he thought a few crappy epigrams excused him. If that's what passes for love in France, it's all a bit sickening and false. I felt literally sick as I finally closed that bloody book. I'm not sophisticated, Elodie. And I don't want to be."

Elodie takes her arm away and says she's really sorry:
"It was just an impetuous thing."

Now she's the one looking hurt.
It wasn't a row exactly, but it feels like one.

11
First Night

We spent the last night together.

I was leaning with my back against the kitchen sink, wearing only my shorts and boots. Grimy and sweaty and tired.

It must have been half-six and I was done-in.

Elodie came in barefoot and wearing her pale blue cotton dress.

She said it seemed ridiculous for me to ride back to my house when I was so tired and would be here again so soon.

She stood right in front of me, looking me in the eye.

"Please stay", she said.

I looked into her eyes for a long while to be sure I had understood, then slowly put my hands around her waist. Her dress was smooth and it felt good when I rubbed it gently against her body.

I smelled her scent and her skin and we slowly kissed.

She tasted of summer and wine and tobacco.

I said that I needed a shower but she said no.

We went upstairs and into her room and she drew the curtains so we were in half-light.

I could sense she wanted me to lie absolutely still.

She was in charge. That was fine. She kept only her dress on.

She explored my body—almost as if there might be questions afterwards. Maybe I was briefly her dead husband. I didn't much care. She ended up on top of me. Transformed. Here, but elsewhere too.

She changed her legs as she would when riding. Long stirrups and short stirrups, until she ended up almost squatting, knees up.

She was concentrating hard when I burst inside her. She was almost laughing, but also sobbing, as she fell on my chest, her wet hair in my face.

Unrequited sex.

And then this morning, as the birds started to sing, it was the same.

(I mean exactly the same.)

Today, I can't stop thinking about it. The sheer joy of it.

As Elodie lay beside me afterwards, she said not to worry.

It would be my turn next and we could do whatever I wanted.

And she put her arm across my chest and slept again.

12
Random Harvest

It's been another hot day, but the evening breeze is sweeping in.

After I shower and change into navy shorts, white plimsolls and navy rugby shirt, Elodie reminds me it's film night in the village and she has to make an appearance. I don't ask why, but I do ask what the film is.

She looks again at the *Village Voice* flyer on the kitchen table and reads out: "*Random Harvest*. 1944. Ronald Colman and Greer Garson star in this classic romantic drama."

"Sounds hilarious," I say. "Can I come too?"

(I think we're already seen as a couple in the village. In the shops, I mean.)

As we walk to the far end of the village, Elodie links my arm. This is somehow my favourite feeling.

The cool breeze is refreshing. To her surprise, I recite *Sensation*, by Rimbaud. It seems to suit the moment. She says bravo and does a little clap.

Then I start doing my 1940s English toff accent to amuse her. I love old films. When she's stopped being amused, I still continue awhile. But just for my own amusement. (A failing of mine.)

As we arrive at the black wooden Scout Hut, we see a gathering of mostly white-haired people outside, all looking very smart. The couple in charge greets Elodie warmly and me with undisguised interest.

The evening is bright, and blackouts have been drawn. It adds to the faintly wartime atmosphere. Motes hover in a bright crack of sunlight.

We sit together and it's the most wonderful, joyous feeling.

The screen flickers into life.

In the dark, Elodie's scent smells like after rainfall.

As the story unfolds, I am completely absorbed.

Ronald Colman is a casualty of World War One and has total amnesia.

He's like a child in an orphanage waiting to be collected, but who never is or ever will be. In fog and confusion on Armistice Day, he escapes into town and is found and then protected by Greer Garson, who plays a vaudeville actress.

They form an idyllic attachment and marry. They even have a child.

But when he goes by himself to Liverpool for an interview, he gets run over and is again concussed. This time, he has forgotten everything *since* the first injury. He thinks the war is still on. He returns to his rather aristocratic family, who had believed him dead, and becomes a successful, but lonely and remote, captain of industry.

In a *coup de théâtre*, his highly able and business-like PA appears and she is his forgotten wife, Greer Garson. She is not permitted (on psychiatric advice) to tell him the truth, so he just works with her without recognising her.

The point is that he sees her and hears her but he doesn't recognise her.

He can see her but can't really see her. Because his mind can't see her.

Even though he somehow still loves her, his love is buried and lost.

Only when he somehow re-enters time at an earlier point and becomes his old, forgotten self can he recognise her and release that hidden love.

Time is unwound.

Perception isn't enough. That idea seizes me. His senses aren't enough.

There is some forgotten template he has to retrieve and use to cut out the shape of his lover from a raw, anonymous experience. That's his task.

And he can't recognise her inner self until he has rediscovered his own.

As the film ends, we walk out into the night air, shouting our goodbyes and lots of white heads float off like jellyfish into the blackness. My high spirits have been replaced by utter seriousness, but I've probably never felt happier.

I can't explain to myself why the story grips me so much. But that's exactly why it does. I recognise something, like a silhouette, that I can't dredge into the light of consciousness and that's what the story is about.

Elodie asks if I am OK and I say, "Yes, more than OK, thanks. That was great."

And we walk home quite silently, arm in arm, under a greenish sky.

13
The Opposite of Murder

We're lying naked in bed and it's late. I'm face down, arms folded.

The sash window is open to let in the breeze. Elodie is sitting up and smoking, the sheet tucked under her arms, an ashtray in her lap. She's staring straight ahead.

"You know when things started to go wrong between me and Henry? It was when we found out that I couldn't have kids. That seemed to change everything. We hadn't thought about it or talked about it. But when something is taken from you, you feel the loss. Even if it was something you never had. Where I come from, women are like fields men plough and sow. It's seen as such a shameful thing, being...But you know, I'm not sure I ever really wanted children. I might have made a lousy mother. Have you ever thought, Fergus, that having a child is the opposite of murder? And just as serious. Dragging someone into all this without asking them first. Murderers get twenty years and parents, about the same. But in this village anyway, I think few serve their time. They get over the wall. The men especially. And I don't think I could have lived with that, either. Having a child and being a rubbish mother. Or maybe being abandoned. It was after this discovery that I started to lose Henry. Little by little. Then all at once."

14
Planned Harvest

We're in the garden in the shade. It's almost dark. The candles on the table are beginning to the gutter.

"Elodie, you told me once that you were Catholic, but that's not true."

"Well, I only meant that where I come from, everyone is. We'd go to Mass and afterwards stand outside as our tenant farmers said good-day and doffed their caps! Marrying an English Protestant wasn't really on the cards. But I'm not a believer. It slowly dissolved in my teens, I think."

"So you don't think there's a divine plan or anything? No grand design?"

Elodie looks askance at me and then seems very serious.

"Only a plan by a monster, maybe. Look at the world, for goodness' sake."

"But maybe God is giving us opportunities to help people—"

"Then he has Munchausen's by proxy," she snaps back, angrily.

"But some people think it will all make sense in the end. In the next life—" I weakly offer.

Elodie looks at me and says, "On my eighteenth birthday, I was given a small present at breakfast and a card. (My birthday comes at harvest time.) There was no fuss at all. Then we all had a busy day on the farm, working flat-out, as you say. Then in the evening, I trudged upstairs for my bath. Mother had laid out one of my nice summer dresses on my bed. When I came down, the house was full! They had arranged a surprise party, with all my friends and workers and our family friends. And they presented me with a cake and an expensive necklace."

"Why are you telling me this now, Elodie?"

"Because I remember that day of misery and the feeling of being unvalued much more than I do the party. It's still there in my past." (She clutches her heart.)

"That stupid party didn't wash it away. It meant only that I had the feeling of foolishness to add to the feeling of hurt. They didn't know me. That's what they were somehow telling me. But also, they robbed me of my freedom for a day. Welcome to adulthood. When you lie and deceive, you stop the other person from being able to truly decide. You hide some of the cards. I don't think even God can fix what I see every day on The News. It's there forever."

"I think you may be a *lapsed*-Catholic Elodie," I say, looking at her knowingly.

At this, she laughs out loud. "And you're not, I suppose!"

She's found her lightness again. The moment has passed.

"Now tell me about your eighteenth, Fergus. What did you do?"

I have to think to answer.

"Nothing at all," I say. "It was just another day."

15
Judgment Day

It's finally results day. I'm not remotely nervous as my grades don't matter that much. Birmingham, King's and UCL all made me two E offers. James, on the other hand, needs impressive grades.

We've arranged to meet in the village, here in East Haddon, in the garden of The Wheatsheaf. James hinted he'd like to meet Elodie and I've warned her we might come back up to the house.

It's half-eleven and I've phoned the school. It's fine. Three Bs and a C.

That's more than fair, considering my antics in the Upper Sixth.

I've already left a message in Cork, at Uncle Jerry's place. Mum and Dad will be pleased, I hope.

In the pub, I order a Coke. Lots to do this afternoon.

I wander down to the shady end of the garden. James is always late.

When he shows up, it's good news. He has a drink in one hand and his crash helmet in the other and he's grinning.

"All well with you, old thing?" he calls out as he approaches me. (People stare.)

"You bet, James. More than happy. How did you do?"

"Straight As, old boy. Overjoyed. All that graft paid off and all that guff. The Winko practically burst into tears when I told him. Mum too. She sends love, by the way."

"Send her my love too, James." (I like Helen.)

I congratulate him, and he me.

James proffers a gasper and I take one and we both light up.

As usual, we set about swapping memories. Correcting one another as we go, never reaching an authorised version and never really wanting to.

James did English Lit., French and History. It was his dynamic young history teacher, Dr Snowden, who got him organised for the Oxford entrance exams and encouraged him all around, really.

I did English Lit. and French too, but with Religious Studies.

Art was very much on the side. (For recreation, almost.)

I hadn't done O-Level Art, but my handful of sketches proved enough to get me onto the course.

I hadn't done Religious Studies either, but having been informed that most of the course was philosophy and ethics, I applied for that too and was accepted. I even got to like the other stuff: creeds and heresies.

Obviously, I was going to take English Literature, especially once Selkirk had left.

(Not that I was much good at it, but by now, it was a family tradition.)

French was nailed-on. *Les Mains Sales, La Gloire de mon Père, La Chute.*

And Mr Lewis, though far from flashy, always got everything across.

We review the last two years as if to put them behind us.

There were three people in the Art and Religious Studies classes, and about seven in English. The survival rate to even get as far as the Sixth Form bore comparison to that of a 1917 airman.

Perhaps these enviable pupil-teacher ratios meant we could finally expect an absolute blast.

Perhaps our teachers had been conserving themselves for this exclusive coterie.

And perhaps not.

I decide to go first and to have a good vent. James ostentatiously listens.

Art was taught by a man, Mr Carlisle, who was notorious for the extra attention he was prepared to offer certain girls. The boys were very much in the way, in fact. He had the unapologetic air of a whiskery Ealing Comedy cad.

But he could paint, after a fashion, and did so in class. He didn't demonstrate or teach painting; he simply painted his pictures, for private commissions, in our lessons. Landscapes, steam trains, Spitfires. That sort of thing.

The other art teacher, Mr Newman, was a brilliant artist, who had, incredibly, exhibited at The Royal Academy. He wore a seraphic smile and his dark blue eyes seemed to look inwards, rather than out. He spoke in a whisper, possibly to conserve energy, which seemed a rather pressing matter. In lessons, he would spend much time slowly sorting out large drawers full of coloured paper. He did this with a quiet intensity that was slightly disconcerting.

The only practical guidance came at the end of a session, when he would look at your painting, form a little oblong with his fingers and thumbs, squint and frown.

"I think this bit's working," he would say, waving at an arbitrary area before returning to the drawers.

Perhaps he'd lost something.

The three of us pupils were left to our own devices. We didn't know, or have a copy of, the syllabus. We simply set up tedious still-life arrangements and painted them on cheap paper with stodgy acrylic paint.

Only in the final few weeks did the staff confide to us the exact course requirements. Frantic efforts to conjure up pastels, charcoals, figure drawings, designs and even some short essays eventuated in the kind of portfolio that would make any visiting examiner ask cheerily for a brief coffee-break, before slyly calling The Samaritans.

Religious Studies was also a bit of a facer. Mr Evans was chapel, pronounced CHA-pel. He was from the VAL-leys, from a mining area. A bachelor who still lived with 'mam', his not infrequent domestic references evoked *Psycho* more than *How Green was my Valley*.

Mr Evans was generally dismayed with the way history was unfolding and made dark pronouncements to that effect: "The unITED Nations is a more DANGerous institution than The KREM-lin," he would opine, chalk breaking in his hand.

"Evolution is only a theory, see. Pure THEE-ory," he would add, welling-up.

(The Whig view of biology, presumably, and not to be trusted.)

We never got onto the shape of the Earth, but his take on that would have been equally intriguing, I don't doubt. I think he was unwell. Certainly too unwell to conduct us safely through the ontological argument, or explain the implications of the *Euthyphro* dilemma or the Marcion heresy.

(James and I both lapse into Welsh accents at this point and find it hard to stop. As I continue my rant, he keeps muttering: "They gave of their NOTHING." which cracks me up.)

English Lit. was endurable not because of the teaching but because of the texts:

The Wife of Bath, Measure for Measure, Murder in the Cathedral, The Complete Plain Words, and, rather inexplicably, *Corridors of Power*.

(Which shit of an examiner thought we'd care about the lives of senior civil servants, I cannot imagine. I never finished reading the bloody book, but listened attentively to James' account of it instead.)

Mr Morris was nearing retirement and had, like the others, little experience of teaching A-Level.

A humane and basically harmless man, he could wander.

Lessons included his part in the liberation of Belsen at the end of the war and the fact that a friend from school days had contracted gonorrhoea ("…and don't give me any of that guff about toilet seats, either"). Also, the necessity for him, when a student, to read racy books in the village churchyard, his mother being "Very particular about smut, see." (Lawrence, most likely.)

He must have had some kind of wall chart, as whenever we read Chaucer around the class, Amy Berridge, the school prude, would invariably get the passage containing the Middle English for cunt, prick or fuck. I'm afraid we enjoyed her unease, there being too few amusing things to rate it against.

Although we don't remember any stimulating discussions at all—not one—in any class, there were, of course, many to be had with fellow students in the tiny but ample Sixth Form common room, which was—inevitably—a mobile classroom.

Everyone who remained in the Upper Sixth was an autodidact, after all.

At least here, we could play records, read the *NME*, weep, confess, advise, flirt, warn, enjoin, kip, snog, commiserate and laugh. Two years in that room would've been more profitable without those pesky and highly inconvenient lessons.

We hadn't been a year group so much as an escape committee.

My vague and clearly unsupported plan to go to art college disintegrated when I decided that a foundation year before leaving home was more than I could bear. I needed to go.

No one in the last year had discussed the next step with me and I, clearly, had not asked. I was one of the last to apply to university.

I suddenly remember that James changed his image in the middle of all this and one day appeared dressed entirely in denim: jeans, waistcoat, jacket. (He'd have worn a denim cravat if they'd sold them.) He'd also had his hair frizzed in a style any friend would recognise as more a cry for help than a fashion statement.

He revoked this image just as suddenly one day and resumed the Young Rotarian look.

It was as if it had never happened. A fugue of some kind I expect, and something we never spoke about—until today.

(James cringes. Excellent.)

When he was applying to Oxford, he had worked hours that would cause a walkout in a Shanghai sweatshop, I remind him. Thought I'd lost him. Yet, he was still finding time for the occasional Sobranie Black Russian and a Waugh novella.

Then one day he returned, but now as one who had, unlike the rest of us, seen over the horizon, like Moses.

James accepts most of this as forensically sound, as he puts it.

Unlike me though, his fondness for the place seeps into his own version.

I let him ramble on for a while and then say, "Stockholm Syndrome, James, plain and simple."

James pretends he feels unfairly rebuked, then he tells me about his Caribbean holiday. Far safer. And very Noel Coward.

Before we leave, we do our usual thing and scan the clientele.

The silent couple who are planning to murder the man's pushy mistress.

The fat man who dresses as a Nazi on Sunday evenings as he listens to Wagner.

The virile young man who works on a building site and goes by himself to Sadler's Wells twice a year.

As we leave the pub, James asks if he can see where I'm working.

When we reach the lawn, I see Elodie sitting at the garden table.

She's bought a homemade sponge cake from the Co-op and a bottle of sparkling wine.

(Blue gingham sleeveless dress and navy court shoes. Elodie must know how much I notice what she wears. She's always so chic. And also what she doesn't wear. No rings or jewellery. Except for her drop-earrings: some of ivory, some of peacock feather.)

After the introductions and congratulations and passing around of cake and glasses, Elodie and James talk for quite a while, as if I'm not here.

"Compiègne? But we have friends in Compiègne! The de Vaals. You must know them. Arty types."

"No. I'm afraid I'm a country girl. Sorry, James."
Then soon after, "Henry Fleetwood? Didn't he hunt with the Pytchley? He must have."

"Yes, actually."

"And you? I suppose you did too, Elodie."

"No. I ride. But I don't hunt."

"He must have known *the Hamiltons*!"

"I really don't know, James. Our friends were quite separate, really."

After he's gone, she turns to me and looks suddenly tired.

"Your friend is surprisingly coarse, I think. And acting. Always acting."

She starts to clear the table, and I help. The wine was hardly touched.

"Am I coarse, too?" I ask.

Elodie looks at me, mock-gravely.

"'Course not," she says and beams at her *double-entendre*.

16
The King Is Dead

Elvis died yesterday. It's all over the radio. The women in the Co-op were talking about it and one of them was crying inconsolably.

When I get to work and walk into the kitchen, Elodie is in a rare old state.

"Oh my God! This Elvis thing is crazy! It's totally out of hand."

I unhelpfully say he was probably bigger in Britain than in France.

She glares at me, hands on hips, knife in hand.

"I just heard this record on the radio. I listen to the words. Does anyone else? Listen? *She's everything a man could want, but she's not you.* She's exactly the same as his girlfriend but not good enough? Really? It's so preposterous! If she's the same, he should love her too, for goodness sake. Why ever not? If you fell in love with one identical twin, you should love both, no? If they're truly just the same, I mean. If you love one and not the other, you are just—insane. Can't we love types? I think some people do! We can be faithful to a type. And when the individual stops being that type because they get too old or whatever, that's too bad. And if you move on to a younger model who is more that type, you're not being unfaithful because you're still being faithful to your type. Which you love. Do you understand me?"

There are tears in her eyes.

Possibly, yes, I suspect I do. But I don't say so.

17
After the Ball Is Over

After our late-evening drinks and some barefoot dancing on the lawn to Nat King Cole, Elodie lies on the tartan picnic blanket and stretches her arms above her head, her legs slightly apart.

The garden is lit only by a line of candles in the kitchen window.

"Come and be with me," she says, sleepily. She's wearing a white cotton sleeveless shirt and a pleated navy skirt.

I lie down beside her and pin her arms down.

We kiss a long kiss and as I slowly pull up her skirt, the satin lining rustles and she opens her legs still more. I stroke the back of my hand against her left thigh, then I sit up and plant my hand on the ground between her legs and face her. Elodie sits up too and puts her forehead to mine. I can feel her pushing herself tight against my wrist.

I whisper to her about her all the things we shall do and where we shall do them.

Elodie lies back on the blanket and folds her arms over her eyes as if shielding them from the sun.

18
The West

I'm in Slaney's Bar in Westport. It's mid-afternoon but practically dark, as the rain lashes down outside. When the wind turns, it sounds like gravel being thrown against the window. The slates on the roof mutter something under their breath every now and then. The Wolfe Tones are being played on the jukebox. *Only Our Rivers Run Free.*

I wanted to get to Ireland at the end of the summer, even though it's only for a few days.

I've already been in the back room where the teenagers always are, but I'm suddenly too old. And the place reeks of weed.

Last year, I sat there on the sofa with the two Slaney girls and got a good lecture on New Wave music and life in New York. God, they mocked me. But they're not here anymore. Got their Green Cards.

Eilish and her squeeze, Daniel, are both here in the front bar, by the potbellied stove. Eilish admires my beard and strokes it approvingly.

She's extremely pretty and looks Jewish: even her Jewish friends say so.

Daniel looks like an Arctic explorer. And I, like an inmate at Long Kesh.

We've all noticed that our accents are going down really badly this year.

But there's no chance of any of us apologising on that account.

We're used to being in the unwelcome minority after all. We like it.

Daniel's a bit shaken up. Yesterday, he went for a walk over the Sheeffry mountains and ended up in a hidden dip. The IRA was there doing firearms drills.

He thought about running, but they'd seen him and it wasn't a good idea, anyway. But they held him for hours and one of them went up to the farm to see Uncle John before they would let him go—with a heavy warning to say nothing.

A warning he's ignoring by telling me about it. In a pub. As men nearby are watching us. Brilliant.

We still manage to laugh. We always do.

They tell me about their travels. They've been here in The West all summer, driving up and down the coast going to races and festivals.

At one point, Daniel says he's thinking of moving here.

By the way, Eilish looks at him, it's the first she's heard about it.

(I imagine they'll return to that one later on.)

I tell them that I spent yesterday at Thallabawn, by myself all day.

Miles of soft white sand and views across to Galway and the islands.

I took Descartes' *Meditations* and read them on a headland. As I got to the end, I saw a pod of dolphins. I watched them play as the sky turned red, and thought of my relatives in America. As kids, Redmond and I found the jawbone of a whale in the sand here. And a lollipop stick from New York, with a baseball Q&A written on it, one on each side.

I was miserable that Elodie wasn't with me. All joys are halved. More than halved.

She's everywhere but as an absence or a silhouette.

After a while, Michael, my cousin, who is my age, joins us. (Pale blue eyes. Always looks as if he's struggling to keep a big secret.)

The round table is almost covered with fresh pints of creamy Guinness.

We always catch up pretty swiftly. He tells me he's driving over to Killary Harbour very early in the morning. If I want to come, I'm welcome.

He has to pick up some crabs and lobsters and deliver some to Delphi Lodge and some back here in town, at McDaid's restaurant.

Sounds good, I say. Though not thrilled by a 6 o'clock start idea.

***

I'm feeling crapulous as I knew I would, but it's a lovely morning after the stormy night. Blue sky. Turf-fire smoke. The call of seagulls.

As we get into the white Ford van, I can see Clare Island in the distance.

Michael drives way too fast, but we touch the road now and then. Soon we're passing Doo Lough, where so many died during The Famine.

It's bleak in any weather.

On our left, we see Ben Gorm, then The Devil's Mother and Maumtrasna, on through Leenaun and turn into the hidden boreen to Killary. Only one car can pass here. Lough Fee on the left.

After about six miles, we can see the fjord again. It had been hidden by the low hills to the right. Soon after that, we drop down to the shoreline and after another mile or so, by choppy water, we get to the harbour. There's almost no room to turn the van, but Michael manages and we get out. This is Rosroe. Next stop, Boston. Still only six-forty.

We'll be here for half an hour or so. Michael heads off to see a couple of boatmen and I walk up the path to get a better view out to sea. The water is turquoise and dark blue and sage green. As clouds pass, the colours change and distant strands are lit up and then darkened again.

On the other side of the fjord, Mweelrea looks sheer. Our sheep go up there and have to be shepherded back every few days.

I see a line of about four white cottages. This is all there is to Rosroe.

One has a small Youth Hostel sign over the entrance and is open.

I step inside the hallway and sense that any visitors have already left.

There's a (probably collectable) drinks machine and I manage to get a black coffee, of sorts. As I turn to leave, I see a small bronze plaque above the door:

Ludwig Wittgenstein, philosopher, stayed and worked in this house at various times from 1934 to 1948.

I don't know anything about him, but the name seems familiar.

As I walk further along the path to the bench at the very end, I see an old man with a collie returning to his cottage. They both go in and he closes the bottom half-door, leaving the top half open.

I slowly approach the door and, hearing my own accent as very English, I ask the man (who's by now sitting down just inside) if he remembers the man who stayed there during the forties.

He gets up and steps towards me.

"I do remember him, well, of course," he growls. "And he was a madman!"

And with that, he slams the top of the half-door shut.

I suppose he has all the company he needs up here, without mine.

On the way back, Michael insists we stop in Leenaun for a pint.

It's seven-thirty and we have two each, before resuming our errand.

We'll be home for breakfast by nine.

***

In the evening, when I'm speaking with Uncle John (by the elms and beech trees that half-surround the farmhouse) I ask about the philosopher. Grandfather knew him slightly, apparently. He said Wittgenstein tamed the wild birds so they would eat from his hands.

But after he left, the cats had them.

Being tame made them easy prey.

19
Last Days in East Haddon

We're both back. (Elodie has been away too, up North. It's still her plan.)

We have plenty to talk about. Six days away felt like much longer.

(Is she dressing down? No, that's absurd. But if her chocolate-brown sleeveless blouse and long brown crepe skirt were meant to deter me, the plan isn't working.)

She says she's ready to get an estate agent in. We walk over to the place together, discussing what remains to be done.

The stables are finished, both the whitewash and the half-doors (dark green). The stone floors are scrubbed. The courtyard cleared.

I haven't touched the kitchen or Elodie's bedroom, but have painted the other three bedrooms, the sitting room and the hall.

The limes are well cut-back and the vegetable garden mostly dug over.

It's deceptively big, but provided a good work-out.

***

The estate agent has brought a photographer with her.

She's enthusiastic but business-like. Optimistic, but realistic. Got it.

Elodie allows the photographer to go everywhere but her bedroom. It's quite a bright day and both house and garden should look great in *Country Life* or whatever they use.

When it's done, the four of us sit in the kitchen for a late morning coffee.

The estate agent, Abbie, becomes surprisingly chatty. I don't know if it's the caffeine, but she's soon hooting and seems ready to go out on the town. She used to be a teacher. Geography. Her husband was the estate agent but he's moved to Spain with one of her old friends: their bridesmaid in fact. "Life, eh?", she offers plaintively. Then she regains herself a little and adds, "I'd welcome her back, mind. Not him though. Never." And hoots again.

She's taken over his agency and has several employees. Much happier. She's hoping to retire within the next ten years (she's about mid-forties) and move to Australia or Florida. Abbie came up here from Surrey. No ties.

I don't think the photographer has heard the husband bit before. He looks rather surprised. Perhaps he's disappointed he's not working on Fleet Street.

Abbie tries to get Elodie to reciprocate with a brief life story, but it's clear that's not going to happen. I like the way she evades and distracts without being rude or making Abbie feel a fool.

When she knows she's drawn a blank, Abbie looks me up and down as if I don't quite belong here.

Whatever you say, say nothing.

Yesterday, I was in the kitchen at the sink, guzzling a cup of water after too long out digging. Out of the corner of my eye, I saw Elodie come in. I didn't even know she was home.

As I turned round, she sat on the kitchen chair and looked at me.

She was wearing a knee-length, lemon-coloured linen dress I hadn't seen before, with narrow shoulder straps. It looked expensive.

"You look as if you're in a bit of a state," she said.

"I'm fine," I replied.

"No. I can tell. You're in a state, I think."

She caught hold of my belt buckle and drew me towards her and started undoing it.

"Permit me," she whispered, looking into my eyes.

A few minutes later, she was leaning on the table and I was behind her and inside her, crying out, holding her narrow waist under her rucked-up dress. This rough magic.

Afterwards, I ran my hand up her back to the nape of her neck. My legs were sea-legs by now. I almost fell.

She turned around and clasped me in her arms, saying, "Kiss my mouth." And we kissed for the longest kiss ever.

And when we separated she smiled and looked down at the front of her dress, holding it up to the light, even and mock-complained she'd have to change it, now.

She didn't though. She wore it all evening.

Today I'm working, but thinking only of yesterday.

Elodie is out, in town.

She knows I'm going soon.

Is she saying goodbye?

Or don't go?

I work from nine until about half-eleven, but then Elodie says that's enough and we go inside and lock the door. We spend the afternoon in bed, with Georges Moustaki on very low, curtains drawn.

I get the impression that Elodie has no idea how deep my feelings for her run. Annoyingly, she's been doing the sophisticated older woman act for a little while now. Trying to be like Lea in *Chéri*, (which was on telly recently). Trying to shake me off.

Apparently, I need to throw myself into university life. I mustn't forget to do some work now and then. Maybe I'll meet a nice English girl. Perhaps I'll change. That can happen. I'll miss the countryside. But London does at least have trees. Of course she'll send her next address. But she doubts I'll need it. Yes, I can write, but why would I? And anyway, I'll be too busy. I'll soon see.

There is some faint mockery in her tone. As if to say: I hope you know what a summer fling is and the rules that go with it.

We try one final philosophical exchange, but it falls flat.

She asks if I had read the *Meditations* when I was away and I say I did.

But instead of telling her what I made of it, I end up simply describing where I sat when I read it, and the sunset and the dolphins playing nearby.

(They chose air and water. We chose air and earth. Who chose best?)

Elodie adds that it's been a lovely summer and she's enjoyed our talks as well as our intimacy. Wouldn't Mrs Courtney be surprised if she knew what her introduction had led to?

I try to say things, too, but Elodie stops my mouth with gold.

Well, my final pay packet, anyway.

"It's been a lovely summer. And it's over. I've ordered you a book, by the way, Fergus. A better choice, I hope."

As I finally leave, I look back one more time.

Elodie is standing with her arms wrapped around herself, in her full-length plum-coloured dressing gown, the porch light on behind her.

Très élégante.

20
Setting Out

Mum and Dad got home yesterday afternoon and I leave for London tomorrow morning.

We're sitting at the breakfast table and taking stock.

They're still not sure. Mum won't move to Cork. That's definite.

Dad might move to Mayo. But I think if Mum actually moves there she'll have to give up the dream-version she's confabulated over the years. She's scared.

Dreaming a dream is fine, but if you actually try living in one, you're likely to fall through the floor. (Unless you're a poet, maybe.)

They both seem subdued.

Maybe they should consider somewhere half-way, like the Isle of Man.

Mother doesn't like my beard. That much she does know.

But it stays, I say.

***

My book from Elodie arrived this morning.

It's the *Journal of Jules Renard*.

Dad drives me to the village station but waits with me until the train pulls in. We shake hands, maybe for the first time ever. No advice, thank God. But he gives me a twenty. A first and last. But that's fine. I have a full grant and plan to live like a Renaissance prince.

I look around in case Elodie is on the platform. I half-expected her to get into the next carriage and meet me one more time before getting off at Northampton or Tring or somewhere. But no.

I seem to feel her absence more than other people's presence.

***

My hall of residence is Brutalist and modern and just off the Camden Road. It's called *Ifor Evans Hall*. (Must look him up.) The walk from the tube station with my luggage nearly killed me.

It's a very noisy and dirty area. Heavy traffic. Newspapers blow in the streets. Greasy spoons. Pubs called The Mother Red Cap and The Dublin Castle. An empty bookshop. Graffiti. Rowdy school kids. Peeling cream paint on the houses. Double deckers heading downtown. Streams of them.

My room is on the first floor, around the corner from the students' bar.

It's fine. Bed, desk, wash-basin, bedside-table, lamp, pin-board.

Oh, yes and translucent orange curtains. (Why?)

I can hear music beginning to emerge from five different directions.

Parents' cars are queuing outside. Quite fancy cars, mostly.

I must get some posters from Athena.

***

21
Bloomsbury

Our first morning in the Philosophy Department has been illuminating.

It's in Gordon Square and I'm sitting with others in the common room on the ground floor, facing the plane trees and the green. The leaves are starting to turn and a few already scrape along the pavement, starting and stopping as they go on their way.

My class must number about twenty-five. An American, a Greek, a Rastafarian, a Pakistani, an Italian, a Frenchman, a couple of Right Honourables, loads of private school types and maybe four or five state-educated ones, like me. I'm one of the very few to have come here straight from school. But everyone thinks I'm older.

My map of Bloomsbury tells me Yeats lived a couple of streets away, in Woburn Walk. The RADA is around the corner, and The Courtauld Collection, on the top floor above the Warburg Institute. Dillons is at the end of the block and the British Museum a ten-minute walk south.

The embalmed body of Jeremy Bentham sits in a glass-fronted case in the South Cloister. He has the face you might find on an old playing card. But too intelligent to be a king.

There are Flaxman reliefs around College and Tonks and Legros drawings and silver-points.

The Royal Institute of Philosophy is two doors down, in the same Gothic building as a private philosophy and theology library I may join.

As I sit here, I'm a bit mortified to remember my interview in the room above: Professor Zeeman's room.

The undergrads I met in the common room, where I waited, advised me to select UCL. I had read *Art*, by Clive Bell, on the train down. The interviewer, who I didn't then know to be the Reader in Aesthetics, asked me what I was reading and I told him. He asked my opinion.

"Well," I said, "It's a complete joke. Bell identified acknowledged masterpieces and spuriously claimed there was a common denominator: significant form. But he neglected to define his terms. And anyway, art is incorrigibly plural."

Silence.

"I see you are doing Art A-Level. Could you comment on any conceptual issues concerning artistic representation?"

After a short pause I hear myself saying, "Let's take that painting on the wall behind you as an example. It's by Nicolas de Staël, I think"—(and on I rant, stupidly, and run dry.)

Silence.

A few minutes later, the tutor, Jolyon Field, thanked me and said I could leave..

A ten-minute interview?

I didn't move at first.

He started sifting through his papers.

I slowly went to the door, grasped the handle and turned around.

"Can't I stay a bit longer?"

***

There's a chap sitting cross-legged and looking at a newspaper by the table. I think he's a First Year too, but he's doing a good job of looking as if he's in his own living room. He's wearing badges on his lapels. Why would anyone do that? Tell strangers what you think, I mean.

He's doing a little floor-show for the rest of us. Lots of tutting. Then he says, quite audibly, that the Army should go in with bayonets and just finish off the Catholics. No-one responds, despite a few looks.

When he gets up a few minutes later and leaves the room, I slip out after him into the hallway and call out, in a friendly way, that he sounds like a fan of political violence. He turns and half-smiles. Then I quietly explain how that kind of thing can backfire. Can cut both ways. He needs to think carefully before he speaks, especially if he wants to keep his top set.

(I hear myself almost as another. My mission to explain.)

He looks a bit shaken, so I let go of his throat and stop pinning him to the wall. He straightens himself up and pulls open the heavy red door and is gone.

Like a trout being released when it's not that meaty.

Stupid fucker.

I stay there for a minute and read the flyers. A Summer School in Dartmouth College. Research grants for the New School for Social Research.

My tutor, Hal Hoffmann, reminds me a little of a dishevelled Atticus Finch.

Rich voice. North American accent. Urbane. Slightly world-weary.

He explains that, as well as being my academic tutor, he's my pastoral tutor also. "Do I know what that means?" he enquires.

"Not really, no."

"Well, it means you're on your own. This is a sink or swim kind of place and I'm not desperately interested in other people's personal problems. Understood?"

"Perfectly."

"Good. That's good."

He then sets me an essay for our first tutorial in three days' time. It's on Utilitarianism.

***

A lot of the lectures are in the L-shaped room where I was interviewed.

White shutters and long sash windows facing the square. Waist-height white bookshelves all around the room. A couple of sofas, a writing desk and a swivel chair, with the de Staël painting behind it.

Others are in College lecture theatres or at Birkbeck, nearby.

I'm getting to make a few friends. Philippa is terrific company and we tend to go to lectures together and for coffee afterwards. I like the way she laughs helplessly. And she points out lots of things I would never have noticed.

She goes to a Freudian psychoanalyst a few times a week, which I find interesting, but never ask about. She loves films and we plan to see loads together, mostly in Camden or at The Screen on the Hill in Belsize Park. (She's always carrying a heavily annotated copy of *The Ham & High*.)

Unlike me, Philippa discloses a lot. (And I mean a lot. I know more about her sex life than I do about my own.)

***

It's late afternoon and I'm in the tiny, squeaky lift up to The Courtauld Collection. It's only two hundred yards from the department.

Some wit has written *Hegel, don't bother me* on the door in black felt tip.

I come here quite often and it's usually almost empty. I love the Degas picture of a lady by a window, and the Gauguin Tahitian paintings.

As I'm stepping back to get a better view, I find myself bumping into someone who's doing the same thing, but in reverse. We both apologise and smile.

She is shockingly beautiful. Luxuriant Pre-Raphaelite hair, partly up in a big clip. She's wearing a long, expensive coat and a scarf, over a rust-coloured dress with a patterned collar. Flat brown suede shoes. Her face is pale and her eyes violet. Scarlet lips. She's carrying a battered brown leather bag and wearing unnecessary velvet gloves. Despite our collision, she seems incredibly composed and smiles easily. I feel rather crass and nothing witty comes to mind.

Nothing that would detain her for a while.

My first tutorial has so far gone better than I had a right to hope.

I just read out my seven-sided essay, in which I tried to include a few *bon mots* and a few solid criticisms, as well as some approval.

Hal was encouraging.

We've just had a very lively conversation. He listens like an owl and gets me to repeat the odd thing to check he's got me in his sights. Which I like.

Before I leave, I mention that I had found it interesting to learn that Mill had a very middle-class English breakdown—one he kept entirely to himself—in his late teens.

Hal makes little secret of the fact that this is, in fact, not interesting.

I add that it seems that what caused it was his imagining that the world was run according to his principles and discovering that he didn't really like the result.

Hal gives me a 'so-what?' look.

I say (rather tentatively) that maybe happiness doesn't make us happy.

Hal is looking at me and clearly wishing I'd already gone, for my sake as well as his. I don't think he's planning on replying any time soon.

"Do you think someone hurt him, Hal?" I ask.

***

I'm in the Donaldson Library. (Very august, indeed.) I always try to sit in the same place, in the far right-hand corner, looking outwards. Once I click on the table light, I enter another world. I'm working on an essay on emotivism.

It's a crackers theory that only a true intellectual would profess and only a dedicated idiot would believe. It's an interesting exercise though.

As I take a stretch and look up, I see the girl from The Courtauld Collection directly across from me, in the History of Art section.

After I stare over for a while, she looks up too and I smile, or try to.

(I end up looking like the Emperor Claudius. I should have either smiled or nodded, but not both.)

She smiles back, fortunately. (But maybe pityingly.)

Undaunted, I quietly walk over to her and ask her if she'd care to join me for a tea-break. She's got a big book on Beardsley open on the desk.

She glances at her watch and says, "Why not? Shall we meet in The Octagon downstairs in half an hour or so?"

"My name's Fergus."

"Mine's Selina."

***

22
Onslow Gardens

We're spending a lot of time together, but I'm keeping an eye on my work. (Selina's a Third Year, so her position's different. Though you'd hardly guess it.)

She's from Northumbria, but you'd never know that either, from her BBC accent. I say to her that she sounds southern.

"Ay oop! Mebbie ah should beh bathin' t'whippits int' front room," she replies quite loudly.

"Careful, your accent's slipping," I say. "That's broad Yorkshire."

I didn't think she'd be funny, but she is. We both laugh a lot, and do impressions. (She's a tough gig though, and can often refuse even to smile.)

She's fascinated by my big family and asks so much about them all that I suspect she's an undercover anthropologist.

She's relatively unforthcoming herself, though. Parents still together.

One brother, a year younger (who, she jokes, she thinks fancies her).

Apparently, he once stole quite a lot of stuff from their home and hid it in the attic while the parents were away for the night. He made it look like a break-in. It was only long after the parents had called the police and claimed the insurance that he owned up. He couldn't explain why he did it. He's at Reading, studying Engineering. Jeremy.

Selina went to some fancy girls' school out in the country. She's never done a job and must know she's unworldly in some ways. But she speaks Italian and German and has travelled all over Europe. She's extremely vain (which is a shame). To the point of massive affectation, in fact.

I don't always believe her. Sometimes, it's as if she's just landed from another planet. And if we go to a pub (which is rare) she always looks around as if she's never actually seen one before. Or a pritt-stick table top, or a dirty glass. All very Princess and the Pea. *Précieuse.*

She's interested in philosophy. Or at least in my tutor and friends in the department. Soaks it up, but doesn't offer that much.

When we talk about art, she's pretty lofty. Dismisses most artists.

Looks theatrically pained when I name the ones I like: Soutine; Orazio Gentileschi; William Nicholson. All unalike.

Likes to quote Berenson. Or Wilde. Or Pater.

Approves of The Aesthetic Movement.

Maybe she should have read English.

***

We usually meet in the hallway of the History of Art Department or The Octagon and go to a café or a gallery. One afternoon, we walked over The Heath to Kenwood House. All pretty chaste, but I don't hide my interest.

But tonight she's just phoned me in hall and asked me to visit her. No reason given and none asked.

I jot down her address on one of the yellow chits in the phone booth and say I'll be there in forty minutes. It certainly beats planning an essay on non-cognitivism.

South Kensington tube is new to me. Rather grand. A film-set feel.

Despite the time of year, it's almost balmy and there's a low full moon.

As I pass restaurants, they smell of the Middle East or Vietnam.

Or at least I imagine they do.

I soon find Onslow Gardens and Selina's address, and ring the bell to the first-floor flat.

There's a buzzing sound and the huge black door clicks and swings open.

The hallway has a black-and-white marble floor and a nude statue of a Greek goddess looking surprised, hands raised to her face. I can't help sympathising, and almost mirror her.

I hear a door open as I ascend the stone staircase and pass the exotic plant.

Selina is standing a few feet inside and says she's glad I could make it.

I ask if everything is OK and she says fine, but does her distracted look, as if my question was extraordinarily intrusive.

The flat is opulent to the point of feeling slightly unreal.

The carpets are deep and cream-coloured. There are Islamic rugs on the walls. A black marble console in the hallway, covered in post. A large mirror above the fireplace, with invitations tucked all around. A mixture of classic and modern furniture. A whole wall of books, many of them late eighteenth century. And at the bottom, a shelf of massive modern books on art, architecture and photography.

The flat smells of expensive aftershave. Leather, patchouli and cedar wood. No TV. No hi-fi. Paintings on every wall. Some old, some early twentieth century. I stop to look at one in a heavy, gold, ornate frame: Saint Sebastian. It has the artist's name on an oval at the bottom.

"Bloody hell. Is this really a Guido Reni?"

Selina condescendingly says, "*Geedo*!" (I had said *Gweedo*.)

"Well, who knows? Studio painting probably. Not my thing at all. Can I get you a drink?"

We go to the small kitchen, which has a shiny emerald green bar with stools and I ask for a glass of red wine from a bottle that's already been opened, and has the cork in.

Selina joins me.

She just needed to not be alone, she eventually declares.

That's fine by me.

We talk and relax and drink a little more.

I ask about the flat and she says it's her father's.

(It crosses my mind that it might not be. I'm naturally suspicious, it seems.)

We talk about College, politics, art, friends, home, films, places.

As it gets closer to twelve and I need to think about the last tube, Selina slips into her bedroom and returns in a white cotton nightdress.

She tells me I can stay the night, but only on the understanding that she's offering her company and nothing more.

I say that's OK. I can head back to Camden in the morning.

As soon as I say this, Selina steps forward and kisses me on the mouth, almost too passionately. She pulls my hair and scratches at my beard.

Soon we are on the sofa. She's unbuttoning my shirt and unbuckling my belt. I'm lifting her nightdress and slipping my hand round her waist. As she continues to kiss me, she manages to whisper that we can't go all the way. Then she pulls her nightdress off over her head and throws it to the floor in a bundle.

***

This morning, I'm drinking black coffee at Selina's kitchen bar.

There is no food in the place, so it's just as well I like it this way.

It's still only seven but I'm irrationally keen to get back to my place and grab an hour's sleep.

Selina meant it about not going all the way. But fortunately, that seemed to leave plenty of scope and we're both pretty knackered.

We're looking at each other more knowingly.

Selina looks like a Whistler model and almost seems to come from that era.

She's wearing only an open kimono, which she clutches together intermittently. I know that when she's dressed, she'll resume the almost prim aura she has chosen for the daylight hours.

She's spectacular. And perhaps unknowable.

As she opens the door to let me out and say goodbye, she loudly puts on the accent of a Cockney tart from an old black-and-white film.

Which throws me a little.

***

23
Soho

I'm in yet another basement sandwich bar with Philippa.

We seem to do this most lunchtimes now, after morning lectures.

I do like her. We met in Dillons, both buying copies of the same book at the same time. She was friendly and familiar in a good way. I was struck by how confident she was. Not really a looker. Long ginger hair. Fringe. Receding chin. Bad skin. Pear-shaped body. Her jacket is too small and her jeans sprayed on. Black pumps. Lives in a modern flat in Highgate that looks like the stage-set of a Beckett play.

Philippa grew up in London. She seems to be quite well connected but doesn't care about all that stuff. I get the impression her parents more or less abandoned her (in a middle-class way) when she was about fifteen. She shows an interest (I do not share) in the private lives of our lecturers. She speculates a lot about them all. Maybe we could turn it into a game, *à la* James. I could try to care.

She wants me to go with her to the cinema this afternoon. It's called *Ai No Korida* and it's on in Soho. (It means: *In the realm of the senses*, apparently. Japanese.) You have to join a club to gain entry. It's that pornographic.

But Art House.

As we leave the pictures, we glance at each other and laugh. It was actually quite interesting. Well shot. Aesthetically pleasing. Evocative of a certain moment in time. Oh yes, and lots of shagging. I'll never see a koan in the same way again. A lot of the sex seemed unwelcome. Or painful. Or maybe rape. Or, of course, it could be just a cultural thing.

We continue talking as the rain starts, lightly at first, then thunderously.

Philippa puts her *Ham & High* paper over her head and starts running.

"Come on! I know a place," she shouts.

A few minutes later, we bundle ourselves into The French House. It's about half-four and almost empty.

We shake off the rain, feeling exhilarated.

"My round," she says. "Do you like Kir?"

"Dunno. What is it?"

To the barman, a balding man with a white handlebar moustache, she calls out: "Two Kirs please, Gaston."

The walls are covered with black and white photos, mostly from the forties and fifties, I think. (One is of General de Gaulle, looking pretty miserable. Elodie would laugh.) We sit in the corner and sip our drinks, which taste sweet, and slightly medicinal.

A few men come in and stand at the bar just beside us. They are exuberant. One of them places two or three large film canisters on the counter. They order two champagnes and a Kir Royale.

"I'll just say hi," says Philippa and approaches one of the two shorter men.

As they talk, he glances over to me. His face goes side to side rather than up and down, and the pink skin is pulled taut like a shiny sweet-wrapper. He nods and points. "Irish are you?" he calls out.

I smile and nod.

"Me too!"

But he doesn't sound it, any more than I do.

He may be the most amused person I have ever seen.

Philippa soon returns.

"That's Francis Bacon. My dad knows him, so I just clocked in."

The tall man has curly black hair and talks a lot.

Monasteries. Liverpool. Waking up in strange cork-lined rooms.

When they laugh noisily at the end of their anecdotes, they can't help glancing over. And we can't help smiling back, approvingly. Even though we don't hear the stories or get the jokes.

Before we leave, I introduce Philippa to the James game.

I nod towards the lady in a leopard skin blouse and black skirt and opine that she drinks her own urine every morning as a tonic.

Philippa then keenly scans the bar and says that the man in the pork-pie hat is keeping his mother's body at home and can't bring himself to report her death to the authorities.

She turns to me expectantly, her blue eyes flashing.

"Good one, Philippa," I say, smiling.

(It's a fine line though, isn't it?)

As I return to the hall, I see about ten police vans in the drive and car park.

The sirens aren't on, but the blue lights are flashing and there are police everywhere, mostly on radios or chatting in groups.

As I walk towards the door I am questioned and eventually let in, where I am not allowed upstairs to my room but directed to the refectory, which is full of students, sitting, standing, drinking coffee. The custodian is here, his wife, too.

The mood is intense.

I soon learn that a student, a Third Year I don't know, has been stabbed right outside my room. He's been rushed to UCH.

There was a huge lake of blood, running under doors, someone says.

Later, it is announced that the young man has died and another student has been arrested.

There is an audible gasp and some sobs and cries.

I'm not allowed up to my room until about two.

I clamber into bed and find my hands clasped in prayer for the lives that were taken and broken only a few yards away and only a few hours ago.

And the families of those young men.

I go to sleep with the overpowering smell of bleach in my nostrils.

***

24
What I Call the RADA

Selina and I went to the Vanbrugh Theatre earlier to see the new RADA production of *Long Day's Journey into Night*.

I thought it was brilliant. We were transported to Connecticut in 1912, and to a recognisable group of people. I found quite a lot of it very funny, much to Selina's discomfort, as I was the only one laughing. Presumably, I was supposed to look intense and reverential. The audience seemed to think so.

Not that it's not a serious drama dealing with serious subjects.

It's just that there's a certain joy in recognition: in-jokes, even.

And also the earnestness of the audience, too. That amused me.

Three hours of sheer enjoyment.

On leaving, I sense a certain frostiness from Selina. She had been embarrassed.

As we walk over to Charlotte Street and then down to Soho, we seem to get further into a deeply uninteresting row neither of us can stop.

(And she seems to be under the impression she's just met my family.)

She's wearing her Slade student outfit, circa 1910, again.

At one point, she says RADA and I say, "It's THE RADA, actually. Ask Peter O'Toole."

At this, she literally stops in her tracks.

"Just what the hell are you talking about?"

"The. The Royal Academy of Dramatic Arts. It needs a definite article."

"Oh, Christ," she mutters and we walk on.

(I know how annoying I can be when riled. It won't change, yet awhile.)

As we sit in The French House, it's all still pretty uneasy.

She's staring straight ahead as if about to walk out after leaving a bomb behind.

There's a commotion at the door as Francis Bacon and his Merry Men arrive. He's completely pissed and clearly ecstatic for some reason. Must have started early. He's telling stories and they're all laughing uproariously, like Vikings. He punctuates one anecdote with a little dance, reminding me of that footage of Hitler outside the railway carriage at Compiègne. Victory.

At one point, he glances over at me and nods. He knows me but doesn't know where from.

A few minutes later, Gaston (looking pretty miserable) walks over and ungraciously places a single glass of Kir in front of me.

I look up and Bacon, his face today like a brown paper bag filled with water, raises a hand slightly, to let me know it was from him.

At this, Selina blushes the deepest scarlet, and glaring at me says, "I hope you don't intend to drink that fucking thing."

The evening has only been a qualified success (as James likes to say).

In any case, it's over, I sense. No Onslow Gardens tonight.

***

25
A Family Affair

It's getting chillier. I walk faster, almost run, as I get nearer Selina's place.

It's been a few days since we last met and I'm hoping we'll just have a good chat and maybe end up in bed together. Maybe laugh about the other evening.

The buzzer is answered by a man's voice, an older man.

(Yes, I'm thrown.)

"Oh, hello. I wonder if Selina is around—"

There is a slight delay, and possibly an exchange of some sort, before the voice returns, "Please come up."

A rather distinguished-looking late-middle-aged man is standing at the open flat door. Aquascutum suit. He extends his right hand.

"Duncan Heatherly. Do come in."

I mumble a thank you and tell him my name.

Once inside, he offers me a seat and a coffee, which I decline.

(There's a fresh cafetière on the kitchen counter, despite the late hour.)

He introduces his wife, who is sitting on a stool on the outside of the counter, smoking. Her legs are crossed and her face looks like thunder.

Chanel suit. Court shoes. Expensive hair-do. Big rings.

She barely acknowledges me and looks away.

"And how can we help you—Fergus?" he asks.

"Well, Selina and I are friends. I was nearby and I wondered if she'd like to come out for a drink—"

There is a pause and they exchange a brief look.

"I wonder—Fergus—and forgive me for asking, but how do you know—Selina. I mean, where did you meet, exactly?"

"We met in the library. I'm studying at UC too, and we met in the College library—"

"Fergus—Selina is not studying at UC, I'm afraid. She's not at all well, you see. We're leaving here tonight to go and see her. She's gone to a place in the Midlands. She needs to get better. Selina has done this sort of thing before."

He looks at me rather sympathetically and decides to continue.

"When Selina was at school, she became heavily involved in drugs, I'm sorry to say. She has developed a recurrent psychosis. She doesn't really know who she is. Neither do we, anymore. She's done this sort of thing in many different places. Abroad even, once. I'm afraid the idea of Selina going to university is laughable. She barely scraped a few O-Levels. She's supposed to be here on a secretarial course."

(Mrs Heatherly—if that's really her name in this crazy place—flinches at this. Disclosing too much to a perfect stranger, I suppose. They're an odd pair.)

"I don't need to know the exact nature of your friendship—all I can say is that the person you have known isn't quite—real. And has probably already gone. For good. To be replaced by another, no doubt. Quite soon."

He looks knackered by now. The poor sod.

I have to think for a minute.

"Do you live in Northumbria?" I ask, solemnly.

"Somerset," he replies, knowingly.

"Do you have a son called Jeremy?"

"Selina is an only child. Our much-loved only child."

He walks me to the door and, as I leave, for some reason feels the need to whisper, "And by the way—her name is *Angharad*."

26
Berkeley

As Hal hands me back my essay on Berkeley, I see he's given me another high grade. Feels good.

He looks at me and says: "I hope you're satisfied that you have grasped Berkeley's big idea."

Reluctantly I say, "I think what Berkeley is saying is pretty clear. It's what it actually means that is less so."

Hal looks regretful-in-advance. (The Germans probably have a word for it.)

"Do go on, by all means. It's your dime," he says politely.

He retreats to the window facing Fitzrovia and looks out. I expect he's thinking of Bertorelli's in Charlotte Street.

I do continue.

"Berkeley is like a kind of Prospero, releasing us from an evil spell. Waving his crozier above his head. He follows the argument to its logical conclusion. He's got guts.

He's made a choice between philosophical integrity and common sense and he's gone with philosophical integrity. It's that appalling bourgeois, David Hume, who says that no one could fault Berkeley's arguments, but no one accepted his conclusions.

But in saying that, Hume just exposes himself as a coward and a collaborator. He puts philosophy aside and sits down with his friends to play backgammon. Ignoring the fact his world has just been dematerialised. Sanctified even. And Mammon, conquered."

"You're not being strictly textual, in my view," says Hal.

"It's about Empire, Hal. The British have asset-stripped Ireland for centuries. Now Berkeley is saying there's nothing left. Or that shit you've already stolen isn't what you thought it was, mate. You've been had. The only remaining gross domestic product is a load of ideas. Dreams. That's all we have left. We're tenants in a world of ideas, not material possessions. There are no owners. Just spectres at a feast of dreams.

It's about greed. Some people are so bloody greedy that they want more than there actually is. They can't understand the word *enough*. Just look at Doctor Johnson. He kicked that rock in an effort to re-colonise the material world that Berkeley had abolished. He suffered *actual pain* rather than give up an idea that literally made no sense and never could have.

If you asked the great lexicographer what the word *matter* actually meant, he would have been absolutely stymied. It means nothing. Never did. But he still can't bear the notion that the Irish are withholding something. Not paying their taxes. Not handing over contraband material substances. Something like that.

When I was a kid, my granny used to say enough was a feast. And here's Berkeley saying the same. Apples are just as they appear and feel, how they taste: nothing more. Don't try to possess things, just *experience* them.

No, no. I've got it. Berkeley has appointed himself as a kind of assistant bailiff. He's thrown the physical stuff out of the house into the yard and said: "Take it. That's yours, that rubbish. Now, let me go back into my house of dreams and just leave me in peace."''

Hal is trying not to look pained.

(I'm vaguely aware I'm being quite loud.)

"Let me put it like this, and I'm just flying a kite here, Hal. Johnson is like someone who bought a Rembrandt and claims to love it. Then Berkeley comes along and says it's not actually a Rembrandt. And Johnson goes fucking crazy and goes right off it. Because he didn't really love the painting at all. He just loved the idea of owning a Rembrandt. Tories like Johnson and Hume don't like ideas that actually change things. Don't you see, Hal, it's all ultimately about colonialism. You do see that, don't you?"

After a long pause, Hal looks over his glasses at me.

"You heard about poetry and philosophy, didn't you, Fergus?"

"No, Hal. What's that?"

"They fell out. Some time ago."

27
Oxford

It's 8 p.m. and I'm sitting in The Bear in Oxford.

I've been waiting here for James for about forty minutes. Is it my imagination or do some of the locals here yearn for their conversation to be overheard? I've already heard enough shite to fill a bucket. If I stay here all night, I'll need a shovel to get out of here.

I'm staring manfully at my book and feigning concentration as I listen to them. So more shite, of a kind. Diogenes would have run out screaming.

I got a postcard from James a couple of days ago.

A picture of a gargoyle with his hands held up to his face, looking appalled (I think). I pinned it to my notice board. He's asked me to visit him. At least, I think that's what he's done.

He wrote only: maieutics urgently required.

Fortunately, he left a phone message at Ifor Evans with a little more detail. So here I am.

And here he is now. Muted smile. Blue eyes sparkling. Tootle scarf.

"Dear boy! Thank you for coming. Much to say and ask."

"Hi, James. Great to see you. Let me get you a drink."

As we talk, I notice that I'm putting away a fair bit of Donnington.

Ebrious, I think, but don't say.

James has finally come out as a teetotaller and sips a pineapple juice.

We talk as easily as ever, but we're also both keen to make some kind of claim to have moved on, learnt, matured, got new material—

Lecturers, work-rates, peers, politics, family news, book reviews, film recommendations, Oxford, Bloomsbury. It flows. *Confelicity. Magpiety.*

I remind myself I absolutely must catch the 8.22 to Paddington in the morning.

As we walk to New College (God, I'm hungry) James assures me that two essays a week is too much and his only recreation lies in evensong and the occasional stroll around the botanical gardens. And Mass, of course.

His room is actually two rooms—a set. No one knows how he got them but he did. We settle into the tiny living room with an armchair and a couch. He's made no effort to adorn the place. History books cover much of the carpet and all of the writing desk.

"I've been keeping this for you," he intones, producing a bottle of wine called *Rouge Homme*.

"Apparently it's the tops, but I'm tone-deaf when it comes to these things, as you know," he adds.

He expertly opens it nonetheless and places it beside me with a glass.

After a few minutes, there's a knock at the door.

"Oh Gus. This is someone I'd like you to meet."

He rises and opens the oak door and a young man confidently enters and extends his hand to me.

"Pleased to meet you. I am Horst."

James, very slightly flustered, restarts the introductions.

"Horst, Fergus. Horst is a graduate student here, Gus. Philosophy."

"Frege, to be precise," adds Horst, effusively.

He's wearing a black t-shirt with white print on it saying: *My Brian Hurts.*

I've got reservations about people who wear jokes on their attire. Especially Monty Python jokes. And especially especially if those jokes fuse together two separate Monty Python references.

I don't think I like him. But I'm also aware I'm slightly pissed by now.

Horst seems keen to be liked and expects to be. He informs me about his life in Munich, and their summer place in the Black Forest. German composers. German philosophers. German cars, even.

If he starts on German measles, I'll have to say something.

James is uncharacteristically quiet, but watchful.

When will this man stop talking?

"I sometimes think all philosophy is merely a footnote to Kant," Horst pronounces.

Oh Christ, I think. And although I've never read a word of Kant myself, offer: "Isn't he the one who invents words instead of actually solving problems?"

Horst looks a little shocked.

"I think one can only appreciate Kant in German, maybe."

"German with little bits of Greek mixed in, you mean?" I add.

He smiles. "Yes, of course, that too."

I continue, "We can't be free but must be. There can't be an objective world but must be. Morality does require a God but, oh no, it actually doesn't. That the fella?"

"I don't think you're being quite fair," murmurs Horst.

"Oh, fuck off," I reason. "Of course, I'm being fair. He was a fucking Prussian, wasn't he? Don't give me *fair*."

(James and Horst exchange a look. Oh dear.)

"And another thing. Wasn't his father a sodding bridle-maker?"

"Well, what if he was, old thing?" asks James, incuriously.

"I would have thought that was pretty bloody obvious," I hiss, and pour myself another red.

After a lull, James says, "You know, I'm a terrible host. Fergus has had no supper. Let me just pop out to the shop on the corner and grab something. Five minutes!"

And he leaves.

Horst turns to me and asks if I met James at Ampleforth.

"No," I say.

"Oh, I thought you were old school friends."

I say nothing.

Then Horst *admits* he's a bit of an Anglophile. And a little starstruck by James' aristocratic background.

(So James has joined the fucking peerage all of a sudden. Perfect.)

"James is pretty good for me, I reckon," he says. "He looks after me, you know. I reckon I'm onto a pretty good thing right now."

I say nothing.

"You know, Fergus, the motto of this College is: Manners maketh man. Isn't that interesting?"

Then more silence.

Only minutes later, James returns, slightly breathless.

"Sorry, Gus. Best I can do at short notice." (What short notice?)

He hands me a packet of Nice biscuits and a brown banana.

"And this is for you." He passes something to Horst.

James puts a record on. Schubert maybe?

As I dip a biscuit into my *Rouge Homme*, Horst starts cutting lines of cocaine on the coffee table. James sits in the corner, just watching.

"You can crash out in my bed whenever you wish, Gus. You must be absolutely knackered. Horst and I will be fine here."

28
Descartes

Hal briskly hands me back my essay on Descartes. He's given me a decent mark and mutters something affirming.

I say, "Hal, almost anyone could have written this, couldn't they? Provided they could read and write, I mean. And get hold of a decent commentary."

"Well, not quite anyone. You're doing rather well, in fact. Isn't it what you actually think? Is that it?"

"Yes, that's probably it." I mutter. "I read the *Meditations* pretty much straight through in the summer and then it came across to me as a kind of modern creation myth, with the six Meditations replacing the six days of Creation."

Hal looks a bit queasy at this and stares out the window towards the Post Office Tower.

"Go on," he says. Resigned by now, to what he is about to receive.

"Well, on day one, we start completely in the dark and gradually discover only a small spark of light. It's pure Gnosticism. God is deposed or forced to abdicate and usurped by an Evil Demon—who claims to be the only rightful ruler. We're never quite sure. It transpires that the world is just a dream. A mental state. There is no matter. The incarnate is made discarnate. On the second day, Descartes discovers he has a soul of some kind, but it's in danger. He doesn't know who to trust. But then, he is mysteriously granted a mystical power—a kind of X-ray vision that allows him to see beyond the realm of the senses…(I hesitate at this as I remember that bloody film I saw with Philippa.) On the third day, God returns in spades. (Well actually, it turns out he'd never really left. Old story.) And he grants Descartes the gift (or the curse?) of the physical world, to go alongside the dreamworld he already inhabited. A second kingdom. On the fifth day, he discovers his soul is immaterial—which he should've worked out earlier, in fact. Oh, and he banishes evil, a bit like St Patrick banishing snakes from Ireland. On the sixth day, the Evil Demon is finally vanquished, order is restored and darkness gives way to brilliant light. On the seventh day, presumably, he rests. By an oven in Neuburg or wherever."

Hal sits down and is looking pretty fed up.
"Anything else?"

"Well, yes. Because there's a secret myth behind the one I just went through. In this one (again, like Gnosticism), it's the Demon who is triumphant. He only *allows* Descartes to think he has won. In fact, you can practically tell when the Demon makes himself invisible. He dictates loads of rubbish arguments against himself and Descartes just writes them down, falsely believing they are his own ideas. One fallacy after another. And he thinks they're great arguments. That's where the Demon hides, in Descartes' certainty. Descartes thinks he's escaped the accursed maze but he's right in the centre of it. On a psychotropic drug supplied by the Demon himself. We still don't know who the good guy is, God or Demon."

Hal looks at his watch, takes off his glasses and pinches the bridge of his nose.

"Perhaps that's an interesting note to end on, Fergus. Interesting note. Until next week then…"

29
The Wallace Collection

I'm having a day off. I've been working hard and I'm tired. And I love being alone, more and more. Philippa says she's worried about me.

(Mutual, I'm sure.)

I walked across Fitzrovia to Marylebone village to see The Wallace Collection. But it's not working its usual magic.

Everything seems flat today.

Before I leave, I look into a small room where there are a few Watteau paintings on loan. The best ones are quite transporting, as usual.

There's also a really uncharacteristic one: *Venus Disarming Cupid.*

(It reminds me of a surrealist painting by Max Ernst: *The Virgin Mary spanking The Christ Child.* Maybe it's where Ernst got the idea from.)

Cupid is getting a good hiding. Venus is clearly a goddess, but not a very powerful one. She makes her plans, no doubt for good reasons, and with the best of intentions. Only to have them wrecked by a much more powerful god, Chaos. Wittily disguised as an airborne toddler.

(Maybe he represents testosterone or pheromones. I heard about a patient who had a brain injury and was in hospital. She used to get up at night and go around the place, changing as many signs and labels as possible. She was quite unrepentant when they caught her. I expect she'd done a lot of harm by then. A kind of Cupid of death.)

I think Venus drowning Cupid might have made a better subject.

As I'm about to leave, it starts pouring heavily. Thunder, too.

I sit in the entrance hall by the lawn. I'm in no hurry and the smell of rain is always good.

I pull Jules Renard's journal from my small rucksack.

I've enjoyed dipping into it. You can start anywhere.

I turn to 1900 and read a few entries.

It says: *The white blackbird exists, but it is so white it cannot be seen and the black blackbird is only its shadow.*

What I like about this is that it says something, but something no one could add to or analyse. It's a magical thought. I underline it in pencil.

As I walk home a little later, along the glossy streets that keep hushing me, I can't help thinking that next time I do see a blackbird, I'll look all around it for its invisible counterpart.

30
Identity

The light is mottled in Doctor Williams' Library in Gordon Square. Stained glass windows and wrought-iron winding staircases. Smell of polish. It's a private library for non-conformist historical and theological research. It's usually empty and certainly none of my UC friends come here.

The essay is on personal identity. It's interesting and I don't know what I think. So, I'm quite happy.

The identity in question is metaphysical, not epistemological.

We're not trying to identify anyone, even though that's interesting, too.

We're trying to map out the properties that underlie any such identification, and that make a person the same person over time.

If Cromwell were still alive and living in Hampstead as a sincere Liberal councillor, would he be the same chap as the scourge of Drogheda?

If Hitler were still alive, but suffering from absolute amnesia, would he be the same man who sent his troops into Poland? That sort of thing.

The identity can't be strict. Everything changes slightly all the time.

It's more like what makes a river the same river over time; change must be accommodated. A change within a permanence. A person who didn't change at all would hardly be a person at all, would they?

So some say, ditch identity in favour of survival. Does enough of me survive such that I can be reasonably considered the same person?

It's not an all-or-nothing issue. It's a more-or-less one. Messier.

I can't see the body as being very important. You could survive a body swap.

And if my mind dissolved, no one would call my dribbling body *me*.

(Well, they might. But they shouldn't.)

I can't see my soul, if I have one, as being very important. It's just a blank sheet. It's the writing on it that matters: that's my mind and me.

But the writing is sometimes applied in invisible ink and is anyway constantly being scribbled out and re-written. And not just by me.

I've changed my mind about God, nationalism, the physical world, free will, true love and the ethics of belief, all within the last few months.

(I'm still a republican, though. There are limits.)

If I'd been born in Bohemia, I'd be a different person from the one I am. But in a way, it would still be me. That *other person* would be me.

But also, wouldn't be.

And if there is someone out there with exactly my thoughts, beliefs and memories, they would be me. Except, of course, they wouldn't. That position is already taken.

Maybe it is just *about* the position. Being in the right place to be who you really are or who you should be. Indexicality (me, here, now) isn't the answer. We're all where and when we are, but that's not enough to make us, us. But how many people get themselves to the exact place in space and time to be their true selves?

(Ipseity may just mean: the right part in the right story. I jot it down.)

I know I wasn't me at school or when I worked at Ferguson's. I even knew it at the time. I was waiting and hoping to be allowed to be me.

Sartre wasn't wrong about everything. It is possible to live a lie. You can find yourself living someone else's life by mistake. Or you can try to find the place you are your fullest self. Your truest self. Your youest you.

It doesn't much matter if you're the same self. (I think they may have got that obsession wrong. Even the watered-down idea of survival isn't very important.) The only thing that really matters is if you are the right self.

Maybe what we are is propped up from the outside, by buttresses, not from the inside, by arches.

Maybe it's other people who hold us together, in some way.

Maybe our true nature is found outside ourselves, in others.

If you want to know about Rembrandt, don't look at his self-portraits. Look at his paintings of Saskia.

31
Post

This morning I found two letters in my pigeonhole in the department.

Glebe House The Green East Farndon Northants

Dear Gus,
    Seasonal felicitations.
    I do hope your term ended as well as it began.
    It was a joy to see you in Oxford, and thank you again for visiting me. I seem to recall that the evening was only a qualified success.
    As your host, I naturally blame myself. It's a curious alchemy. Believe me, you are not alone in so disliking Horst. Everyone does.
    Acidulous boy.
    So you mustn't blame yourself on that score.
    Please convey my good wishes to your family, especially your mother.
    (I do miss dropping in unexpectedly and asking if the kettle is on.)

The Master and I had a little end-of-term chat last week and it was agreed that New College isn't really the place for me, nor history the course.

Too reminiscent of Ampleforth, perhaps.

I shan't be returning for Hilary Term and have already secured a place to read Law at St Andrew's for October.

Belike, we shall meet for a snowy walk in Northamptonshire.

All love,
James

PS. I haven't told The Winko, yet. Yikes! Mother knows, of course.

PPS. Horst is leaving Oxford, too.

And also this:

Dear Fergus,

I hope you are well and that university life is all it should be. You asked me to let you know my new address, so here it is.

Castle Cottage
Coverham Road
Middleham
Richmondshire
North Yorkshire

(I have no telephone.)
Thank you again for all your work in the summer.

I do hope you enjoyed the Renard. A better choice than the first I gave you.

Elodie Loubet

32
Dialogue

Dr Vendler, a College counsellor, is rather tweedy. Fifty-ish.

Very self-possessed. (I should hope so, too.)

Her room is full of books, but the walls are bare, which I find slightly aggressive.

She glances over her glasses at her notepad and says I was referred to her by Professor Zeeman, and adds that most students actually self-refer.

(I'm not falling for that, and say nothing. I'll just take my lumps. I notice my hands are shaking a little, but suppress the urge to light up.)

She gathers that a fellow student was killed just outside my room and wonders how I feel about it.

After the longest possible pause, I outline the view that it's fine by me.

Blood followed by bleach is surely the right order of things. A blessed sacrament.

(I see her scribble.)

I add that murder is no more momentous than childbirth, and I'd hardly be offered counselling if a child was born near my room. (My voice is very flat, I notice.)

Dr Vendler asks if there's an equivalence.

"Only in reverse," I offer. "But in both cases, someone is crossing the divide between life and death involuntarily. Crossing the narrow strait…"
(More scribbling.)
"And, as Socrates said, we don't know who is more fortunate, the living or the dead—"

(My insincerity must be palpable.)

She asks about my personal life and I am willing enough to tell her about Selina. I find I am curiously defensive of her. She was just some crazy positron with a tiny half-life and I was the photographic plate that recorded her spiralling journey.

Hadn't the deception bothered me?

"There wasn't much deception. I had made certain assumptions and Selina then supported them. It had been *folie à deux.*"

Did she remind me of anyone?

"Yes, Ophelia. The Millais one. Not the—other one."
Could I tell her about my family?

"Yes, they're on at The RADA at present. You can get a ticket."

Her look requires me to elaborate.

"Well, maybe my brothers, at least."

I sketch brief accounts of everyone, which seems interminable, but which I, at least, enjoy. They're almost here as I speak.

And my friends? Perhaps I have a best friend?

(I briefly consider Philippa but go, of course, for James.)
"Well yes, he's fictional. But at least not imaginary. He's a character in a 1940s novel. The flesh made word. Slowly swallowed up by stories until no one knows where he starts or ends. He's lost in a good book, so to speak."

(Dr Vendler is increasingly unimpressed by my obscurity but seems unwilling to say much. Maybe she has a counsellor she can unburden herself to. *Ad infinitum*.)

She gets me to talk a little more seriously about James, but I find it hard to do so without fictionalising him further. To keep him from her.

"Tell me about philosophy," she commands.
"Philosophy is essentially cutting," I say. "It's a knife. It's analysis. It chops things up. Anal-Lysis. Breaks things down. But I think it probably needs a fork. Forks *pin* things down.

Forks gather things up. Forks are more feminine than knives, don't you think, Doctor? They look female, compared to knives, which are clearly male. A reclining fork can be a thing of beauty. A Henry Moore maquette. Have you ever you read *Voyage of The Beagle*, Dr Vendler? Darwin has a meal with these Gauchos in Argentina. They're so macho, they eat only with their knives and often end up cutting their own mouths and tongues. Maybe that's what philosophy does. *Whereof one cannot speak...* I'm beginning to have a difficulty in accepting even the axioms of philosophy. The most basic law of logic is self-identity: *Everything is what it is and not some other thing.* But I suspect that's not strictly true. I think maybe everything is also something else, as well as being itself.

Trees are perches. Grass is food. Earth is shelter. Shadows are maps."

Long pause. Scribble time.
"Can you think of anything that makes you happy?"

I murmur: "The thought of a white blackbird. Improbable, but not impossible."

Dr Vendler looks at her watch and is clearly winding this thing up.

"Apparently, you threatened a student at the beginning of term. Is that right?"

"Absolutely not," I say as I comically feign affront. "Some misunderstanding, I imagine. I merely tried to enter into dialogue with this chap and he suddenly dried up and then disappeared. But I was trying to help him. Like a friendly warning to a kid playing with matches. I hope someone might be kind enough to do the same for me in a similar situation…"

And with that, Dr Vendler tersely reads out a few lines of the College policy on bullying, respect for others and freedom of expression.

And she releases me. Into the stream of loonies waiting outside. To have their chakras realigned, or whatever.

33
Blue Train

I'll be on the train from King's Cross to Northallerton for almost five hours.

I didn't know England was so big. I expect it'll stop everywhere.

There are northern accents all around me. (Funny, I never hear them in London.) It's freezing outside. And in, for that matter. I hope it warms up when we get moving. I'm wearing cords and a woollen crew neck. Boots, too. I've taken off my tweed coat, wrapped my scarf around my face and covered my legs with my coat. Everyone is doing something similar.

Cold weather is never expected in this country, is it?

In my rucksack, I have an exercise book and Schopenhauer's essays and aphorisms.

As the long blue train pulls out, I decide not to read, for a change.

Just look out the windows and think and enjoy the journey.

It's been a strange morning. I had got as far as Euston when I suddenly decided not to go home after all, but to visit Elodie.

The cold weather, perhaps.

Mother wasn't impressed, on the phone. Obviously, I lied. Said I had work to finish. (She'll probably imagine I'm in some kind of detention.)

As an exercise, I translate Rimbaud's poem, *Sensation*. I write it out in French, then try different permutations in English. This occupies me for almost an hour, even though it's not a long poem.

I eventually write them out on opposite pages:

Sensation
Par les soirs bleus d'été, j'irai dans les sentiers,
Picoté par les blés, fouler l'herbe menue,
Rêveur, j'en sentirai la fraîcheur à mes pieds,
Je laisserai le vent baigner ma tête nue.

Je ne parlerai pas, je ne penserai rien,
Mais l'amour infini me montera dans l'âme,
Et j'irai loin, bien loin, comme un bohémien,
Par la Nature, heureux comme avec une femme.

Sensation
On blue summer evenings, I roam the hedgerows,
Barley thrashing my skin,
Sensing only
The grass underfoot; the breeze overhead.
I neither speak nor think,
But exult in existence.
Owing and owning nothing, I wander far;
Self-forgetful
As if she were here with me.

I'll show it to Elodie.

She'll say: a translation can be beautiful or faithful, but not both.

After looking out of the window for a spell, I turn another leaf, and start to write.

It comes in lines or in single words. I even draw some images. I find myself arranging them all on a double page. Epistemological poems.

What we know. (Little. Facts are either too few or too many.)

How we know? (Gut, brain, eyes, spirit, touch, sound…)

What we can't know. (The past, the future, if we are really loved, if others even feel at all, if this life is real, if it ends in death, if we are free, if we are answerable, if we are judged, if we can ever learn, how we shall die. Is nature speaking to us? What if it is? The choreography of trees. The Zen garden of deserts. The pulse of the ocean. The music of storms. The wisdom of mountains. The warning of herds. The sparring of hares. The whispering of reeds. The frantic murmuration of starlings: building and disassembling cathedrals in the air. All their pleas.)

We think we're clever, but maybe we're simply deaf. And blind.

I don't understand what I'm writing. I only know that I'm recovering from an illness I didn't know I had.

It's a barely conscious awareness. Just something I see in the corner of my mind's eye. It's as if philosophical questions don't have philosophical answers. Or any answers. But they do have poetic responses. Not full responses. But magical charms, to ward them off.

Not ward them off.
But to acknowledge them.
But in doing so, to stay their hand.
Like Abraham's.
To stop their mouths.
Like Valerian's.
To bring peace.

Questions answered, not with words, but with gestures made of words.

As we pass through Lincolnshire, the snow begins to fall more heavily.

The fields are completely white and the fences are blank musical staves, visually confirming the silence.

By the time the train pulls into the station, I've sketched three poems.

The time went by quickly, after all.

The snow is deep, and Northallerton looks the way towns used to. The bus stop is opposite an Edwardian Art College where the lights are still on. A warm, slightly orange light.

When the bus arrives, it too looks old-fashioned. Smiley-face. Deep green with a bright red stripe along each side.

As I climb aboard and ask for a ticket to Middleham, I admire the red and green seat covers, with red leather trims. Very 1940s. I sit near the back, my rucksack beside me, and look out the window all the way.

It's impossible not to. Mile after mile of snow-blanketed fields and in the distance, but getting nearer, imperious hills.

There are very few people on the bus and they know each other.

We slide into Leyburn and make a stop in the town's large cobblestone square, then circle around and drop into a valley and barely struggle up the steep hill into Middleham. The bus stops at the brow of the hill and the driver kindly calls out where we are, knowing I'm a blow-in and may not be sure.

34
Middleham

As he pulls away and down the other side of the hill, I'm all alone in the village square, or rather triangle. It too is cobblestone, with a few cars parked on it at slanting angles. As the bus disappears in the distance, there is no sound. The snowflakes are big and race to the ground.

There are two pubs, both with inviting lamps on: The White Bull and The Richard III. The benches outside are gently mocked by the snow, now inches deep on them. There are a couple of antique shops, by now closed for the day and, on the corner, a grocery shop with a glass shelter all around, supported by green ironwork. Next to it, a phone box. Everywhere else I see only grey, terraced houses and still further up the hill, a few larger houses. Georgian and quietly complacent.

I walk that way, climbing a slight gradient, hearing only the muffled crush of my footsteps as I go.

On my left, I can just see the profile of the castle against the sky.

Then on my right, a row of tiny cottages huddled together.

Some have outside lamps on, and on one I can see a wooden sign: Castle Cottage.

I suddenly feel rather nervous. Maybe foolish. No phone means no contact.

I may not be all that welcome, for all sorts of reasons—

But I'm beginning to freeze. That always helps make a decision.

I lift the knocker, then let it drop. The sound is like a gunshot and resounds along the street. After a few moments, the heavy curtain inside the door is drawn clear and I see a triangle of yellow light and a silhouette.

I've overlooked how snow-covered I am. My hair and beard are grey.

From the part-opened door, Elodie takes a long look at me before she says, "Fergus, is that actually you?"

"Yes," I reply. "Sorry not to have asked first, Elodie. I was rather hoping you were in."

She tilts her head to one side.

"Up here they say: *Well, you'd best come in*. But I say, welcome."

As I step inside, I leave a puddle in the hallway.

"Let me count the ways," she murmurs, as she takes my soaking coat and scarf from me, and smiles a little.

***

Soon we are sitting by the open fire. The only warm spot in the place.

Elodie is renting the house and the furniture is all at least thirty or forty years old. It somehow looks quite stylish though, because Elodie is curled up on an armchair with a cloche hat on and wearing a Nordic jumper and tweed miniskirt with turquoise tights. We both have huge black coffees in our hands, cradling them for extra warmth.

We talk long into the night.

Elodie has found work, as she had planned, as an agent for several of the racehorse stables in and around the village. They often race in France and she can help arrange the paperwork, transport, lodgings. It's a small start but she's confident it will all be fine. She says she has no money but prefers it that way. I say I have forty pounds in the world and Elodie says, "We're both unencumbered, then."

She asks about UC. I tell her the redacted truth, but still a lot. I make her laugh. I'd forgotten how she shudders with pleasure.

When I tell her about my meeting with Selina's parents, she says, knowingly, "So, a little deranged, then."

I understand the reference and laugh out loud.

I say, "You know, when I was telling you about Boar's Hill, I was so intent on making you smile, but you just wouldn't."

She replies that she thought I was making myself sound like The Lord Buddha when he had wandered outside the Palace grounds and first encountered the Three Sorrows.

Elodie shows me around her house. Her bedroom is the fetch of the one in East Haddon, but much, much smaller.

She shows me the spare room, with a tiny bed and a wall of bookshelves, mostly empty. It's absolutely freezing. I can see her breath as she turns to me and says: "It's alright that things aren't alright, Fergus."

She holds my hands in front of her and looks into my eyes.

"You'd better sleep with me tonight. For warmth, I mean."

***

The next morning, we have bread, butter and jam and milky coffee by the electric fire in the kitchen. It's Sunday, so Elodie is free all day. She suggests we go for a walk over to Jervaulx Abbey.

She slams and locks the door behind us and we walk to the castle and down a lane, past the backs of the houses and their adjacent allotments. There are beautiful horses everywhere, wearing coats and standing stoically on the hard white ground. We walk through three or four fields and reach the River Cover. It's straddled by leafless trees that creak in the breeze as we pass by. Their bark is almost silver. The river is blue and brown and gushes and plunges over limestone flags.

We see a curlew, a fox, some hares.

We walk mostly in silence, watching our footing, our breath visible before us. When we reach the Cover Bridge Inn, it's not yet open.

Elodie says we can drop in, on the way back, for a bowl of soup.

We continue on along the river after it joins The Ure.

Then soon after, we get to Jervaulx.

The sky is cloudless and the snow, dazzling.

We walk quietly around the slighted Abbey. The stones are covered with yellow, orange and green lichen.

On the flat ground, Elodie takes my arm as we walk.

She says that someone up here told her York Minster is like God the Father, but the ruins of Jervaulx are like Christ crucified.

Then she says that she can't understand a religion that has child sacrifice at its heart.

The words child and sacrifice sound as if they have new meanings.

We arrive at a huge fallen tree and sit down, still linked, but looking ahead, through a broken arch, at the wordless land, the vast unpunctuated sky. A few white flakes appear. Then more.

We are in the middle of what would have been the transept, looking west, with wings to both sides. The black foundations can still be seen on the ground, but, as we talk, they are gradually lost.

Whitened by the revising snow.